Seal Secret

Seal Secret

Aidan Chambers

RED FOX

The verse on p. 68 is from "My Mother Saw a Dancing Bear" by Charles Causley and is quoted with the permission of the poet and Macmillan the publishers of his *Collected Poems*. The author is grateful also to Robert Burton for his advice on the habits of the Atlantic Grey seal.

A Red Fox Book

Published by Random House Children's Books
20 Vauxhall Bridge Road, London SW1V 2SA

A division of Random House UK Ltd
London Melbourne Sydney Auckland
Johannesburg and agencies throughout the world

1 3 5 7 9 10 8 6 4 2

First published in Great Britain by
The Bodley Head Children's Books 1980

Red Fox edition 1993
This Red Fox edition 1999

Printed and bound in Norway by
AIT Trondheim AS

RANDOM HOUSE UK Limited Reg. No. 954009

ISBN 0 09 999150 0

1

William stood by the car door and scowled at the cottage.

"I told you," he said. "Nothing but a dump in a wilderness miles from anywhere."

His father humped three bulging suitcases from the car boot.

"One thing you're a world champion at," he said, "is moaning." He piled the cases beside the boxes of food and drink, his own fishing gear and his wife's sun-lamp. "You've not stopped bellyaching since we left home this morning."

"We should have hired a caravan, like we always do," William said. "It'll take forever to reach the sea from here."

His father slammed the boot lid. "Look, Will," he said. "For the last time: your mother wanted a change. It's her holiday too, you know."

"Okay, okay!" William heard the tone in his father's voice that warned of anger on the way.

"She is fed up of being crammed into a caravan with sand getting everywhere . . ."

"All right, all right." William turned his head away and pulled a Dracula face.

". . . and shoals of people all round so she can't sunbathe without being ogled at . . ."

"I know. I *know*."

"And I've got to walk miles to fish quietly."

"And I'm always bringing messy kids in for ices and drinks and meals at all hours. You *told* me."

"Your mother wanted some peace and quiet for a change."

"She ought to get it here," William said, not able to help himself.

"So just stow it, will you, and decide to enjoy yourself."

"I'll do my best," William said, but did not sound as though he would.

His father glared at him. "All right then!" he said, snatching up two of the cases and striding off into the cottage.

"But if I die of boredom, don't blame me," William said when his father was out of earshot.

He slammed the car door and leaned against it.

The sun blazed down. From high in a cloudless blue sky some kind of bird let out a cascade of song that went on and on and on without the bird ever seeming to pause for breath.

"Sounds like this place has driven you crazy too," William said.

In a field on the other side of the hedge that surrounded the cottage and its overgrown garden some sheep were grazing. William stared at them. Now and then one of the sheep would raise its head, stare back at him, and bleat. A plaintive, lonely sound.

"Crazy sheep as well," William said.

Except for the cries of the crazy bird and the crazy sheep there was not a sound. Nor anything in view across the narrow valley but green fields and green trees and thick, impenetrable green hedges.

What a boring holiday this was going to be!

"William dear," his mother called from the cottage door.

William turned. His mother was smiling in the way she did when she wanted William to be nice to strangers and not show her up.

"What?" William said, deliberately unhelpful.

"Come and meet Miss James, sweetheart."

Miss James owned the cottage. Last January she had placed an advertisement in a magazine, offering her cottage for summer rent. William's mother had replied.

William had been against the idea from the start. He liked being right by the sea, in a caravan. A caravan felt more like camping than living in a house. For years they had gone to the same caravan in the same place and always for the second week in August. They saw the same friends, and William knew all the best places to play on the beach and cliffs.

But this year they had come for the first week in September to this cottage lost in Welsh fields half a mile from the sea. All because his mother wanted a change. It was not William's idea of heaven.

"You'll find plenty to do when you get there," his mother had said. "I'll sunbathe all day. And I'll take my sun-lamp and get a tan in the house if the weather is bad. The lamp always does a better job than the sun anyway. Your father will find plenty of fishing because Wales is bound to be full of rivers all over the place. We'll have a great time."

She went happily on, sorting out her sun-tan lotions and bathing suits and the books she wanted to read, while William sat gloomily by. And after that she refused to pay any attention to his complaints.

One thing about William's mother: when she switched off, that was the end. You could cry and whinge for hours, enough to drive most people out of their minds, but she didn't take any notice. She just stuck her nose in one of her books and that was it. Reading seemed to make her deaf.

It had always been like that, from the time he was a baby. William's earliest memory of his mother was of her sitting beside him, reading and paying him no heed.

He knew there was no hope now either. He might just as well go inside without making a fuss and meet Miss James.

As he went in, he saw that the cottage had large red tiles on the floor, old and uneven, and cracked, some of them. He liked them. They wouldn't mind mucky boots. The ceiling was low, with dark wood beams holding it up. The beams seemed to threaten his head. A staircase went straight up from the middle of the room. On one side was a kitchen-dining area, on the other side a sitting-room. The furniture was old and grubby-looking and squashed. (William wondered what his mother would make of that. At home, everything had to be new and spotless.)

The place smelt of wood smoke from a fire in a huge black iron grate that took up half one wall, in a kind of alcove, in the sitting-room. The fire wasn't burning now. The smell was coming from grey ash and half-burnt logs lying in the grate.

Miss James came towards him. She was small and a little dumpy, with white wavy hair cut quite short. She was wearing dark blue jeans and a navy blue ex-service sweater with neat patches on the shoulders and elbows. She looked business-like, almost school-teacherly. But she had a kind face and a friendly smile.

"Hello, William," Miss James said, shaking his hand.

"Hello," William mumbled, not able to hide the embarrassment he always felt when meeting strangers, especially strangers who shook his hand.

"I hope you'll like it here," Miss James said.

"It's all right."

"He'll love it, I'm sure," William's mother chimed in.

Miss James said, "Of course, you'll need time to

settle in. And how about something to drink after your long journey? There's Coke I got specially for you."

"You shouldn't have bothered," William's mother said. "It's more than he deserves. He's been grumbling all the way here."

"A Coke would be okay," William said, knowing he would have to take something. He hoped for some chocolate biscuits with it. Coke and chocolate biscuits were his favourite snack. When he could get them.

Miss James went into the kitchen, disappearing behind the staircase.

"To tell the truth, Miss James," his mother went on, "he wanted to go to our usual holiday place. But his father felt we should have a change. Which is why I replied to your advertisement."

She was speaking brightly and in her voice she used for best, but all the time she was glaring at William in the way that meant: *Wait till afterwards and you'll hear about this.*

"He'll enjoy himself once he's got sorted out," Miss James said from the kitchen.

William's mother mouthed at him: "Behave yourself!"

"I am," William mouthed back.

His mother pushed him sharply on the shoulder.

Miss James returned, bearing a glass of fizzing Coke. But no biscuits.

As she handed William the glass she said to his

mother, "Why don't I show you where everything is?"

Miss James and William's mother went off upstairs, his mother cooing and praising all the way. He heard their feet tread the boards above his head. He felt like a mouse trapped under the floor, and he wasn't sure the ceiling would hold up. The boards certainly sounded thin and creaky.

He drank his Coke in one go, put the glass in the kitchen sink, went to the foot of the stairs and called up:

"Mam, I'm just going for a look round outside, okay?"

"But you haven't had anything to eat yet," his mother called back, "and you haven't changed out of your best clothes."

"Let him go," his father shouted from somewhere behind the sitting-room. By the sound of it, he was in the bathroom. "Get him from under my feet."

There was a moment's silence. William hitched his jeans, then had to stifle quickly a burp from the Coke he had drunk too fast. The fizz came down his nose instead, making him shake his head.

He could hear Miss James talking quietly to his mother; too quietly to pick out what she was saying.

"All right then," his mother called at last. "But don't go far and mind what you're doing."

William fled before his mother could change her mind.

2

Once away from the cottage, William ambled off down the road, back the way they had driven in the car an hour before. It was not really a road at all, but more of a cart-track leading from the cottage to the main road in the bottom of the valley.

High hedges boxed it in on either side, and there was only room for one vehicle at a time. William wondered what happened when two cars met going in opposite directions. As the track was winding, with a number of tight corners: *splat!* He smiled at the crash he saw in his head like a film cartoon.

Already he was feeling better now he was on his own, free for a while. For once, he had not been grilled about where he would go and what he might do and how he might do it. Miss James must have saved him from that, he thought.

After ten minutes walking, though, he began to wonder where he was. The track hadn't seemed as long as this when they had driven up. And he was looking forward to finding something interesting on the main road. He felt more at home on roads.

The tall hedges prevented him seeing where he was. They also trapped the sun's heat. He was beginning to sweat uncomfortably. The tops of trees that grew here and there in the hedge were moving gently, so there must be a breeze above hedge height. Maybe, if he climbed one of the trees, he would be able to see the countryside all round and cool himself at the same time as he took his bearings.

He chose a tree with a smooth bark and plenty of strong-looking branches nicely spaced for climbing.

Getting a start was the hardest. He had to push his way through the prickly twigs of the bushy hedge in order to reach the trunk. Luckily, though, he could get a first foothold on the trunk by standing on a young shoot, and from there he could just reach for a grip on the first proper branch.

He grabbed at it, swung himself up and over, just as if he were climbing a wall. Walls were more in William's line than trees; there weren't too many trees near home but plenty of walls.

But then everything started getting in the way. The buckle of his jeans' belt snagged on the branch as he hoisted himself up. He had to lower himself a few inches to release it and almost lost his hold. He slithered against the trunk but managed to haul himself up again.

This time his shirt buttons caught in some cracks in the bark. He tugged. A button tore off. Then as he swung his leg over the branch, his shoe heel got trapped in the hem of his jeans. He had to wriggle the heel till it came free. In his effort not to fall off the branch, he wriggled his heel too violently. He heard the hem rip.

When he finally managed to sit astride the branch, he was appalled at how much damage he had done to himself in twenty seconds. He pulled his screaming madman face and counted off the ruin.

One button missing. One trouser hem torn enough to leave a loose piece of cloth flapping forlornly. Both shoes scuffed across the toes so badly that wounds of grey leather showed through the brown surface.

Most conspicuous of all, his body and legs and shoes were smeared with a gluey kind of green stuff. It looked powdery, but felt sticky when he touched it. When he tried to brush it off, the stuff spread. He realized too late that the trunk was covered with it, a kind of moss, he supposed.

And he was wearing his best clothes.

"Flipping heck!" William said aloud to himself. "They'll murder me when they see this."

At that moment something small and hard hit him on the shoulder. Thinking a conker had fallen from the tree he looked up, but saw this wasn't the kind of tree that had conkers.

Something hit him again, this time on the chest.

"Down here, idiot," said a voice from below.

A boy was standing in the track. He looked about William's age, but was smaller and knotty in build. He had spiky ginger hair, a ruddy, sunburnt complexion, and wore a tight blue sweatshirt with ragged holes torn in it. His muddy jeans were patched; more patches really than jeans.

"A nice mess you made of getting up there," the boy said. His tone was not friendly.

William tried to look unconcerned.

"What you doing climbing up there anyway?" the boy asked.

"Waiting," William said, trying bravery.

"What for?" the boy asked, suspicious.

"A fool like you to ask what I'm doing."

The boy eyed William for a moment, an unfunny smile on his mouth.

"A clever clogs, you?" he said then.

"If you say so."

"What I say," the boy said, "is if you come down here, I'll smash your prissy face in."

"Charming," William said. He did not feel as brave as he hoped he sounded.

"Wearing your special climbing gear I see," the boy sneered. "Nice that."

William held his tongue. He must not let himself be roused. When he lost his temper, or got nervous, he began to stutter.

"You have no right up there," the boy said.

"Oh? Who says?"

"Me, that's who."

"And who are y-y-you?"

There: it had happened. People telling William what to do always annoyed him. He got enough of that from his parents.

The boy grinned. William knew why. He hitched himself on the branch the better to keep his balance, and gripped hard, trying to check his anger.

"Never you mind who I am," the boy said. "I'm telling you, that's all, see."

"S-save your b-b-breath then."

The boy looked behind him up the track.

"At the cottage, are you?"

"What's it to you?"

"Coming here, treating the place like you owns it."

"D-do you?"

"I live here."

"So?"

"More than you can say, isn't it?"

"Thank g-goodness," William said with as much scorn as his stammer would allow. "It's a d-dump."

"G-g-go back where you c-c-come from," mimicked the boy. "And g-g-good r-r-riddance."

He laughed, mockingly and loud, and ran off down the track.

"English rubbish!" he yelled when he was out of sight. "I'd watch myself if I was you."

3

The row, when William arrived back at the cottage, was even worse than he had feared.

"Good grief, Will, just look at you!" his mother said. "You look like you've been dragged through a hedge backwards."

"Forwards, as a matter of fact," William said, trying to pass off the damage with a joke.

"You *what*?" his mother snapped. The joke was not enjoyed.

But somehow, William could not quell the desire to keep trying. "Forwards," he repeated, though a tremble in his voice betrayed him. "I dragged myself *f-forward* through a hedge."

"Don't cheek your mother," his father said. "You look a right mess."

His mother poked and pulled at his damaged clothes with finger and thumb, as if he were contagious. "I don't know what to do with you sometimes, I really don't."

Miss James stood in the background, looking on but saying nothing. Her presence embarrassed William all the more. He tried to keep his eyes off her, but found nowhere safe to look except at the comfortable red tiles on the floor.

"He's a right cloth-head sometimes, our lad," his father said to Miss James.

"We bring him on a nice holiday," his mother went on, "and this is how he rewards us."

"Thinks we're made of money," his father said. "A good day's work is what you need, my boy. Knock some sense into you."

William counted the cracks in the tiles, trying to keep himself calm. "I was only climbing a tree," he said.

"Climbing trees!" his mother said, her voice rising a note and gaining volume too. "I'll give you climbing trees! You might have killed yourself. *And in your best clothes*. The things I got for you to come on holiday with. *Specially*. Didn't I?" She pushed William on the shoulder.

"Climb all the trees you want," his father said, coming close and bending so that his eyes were level with William's. "Kill yourself doing it, for all I care. I was beginning to think you didn't have the guts. *But do it in your old clothes, dope*."

His father glared at him a moment, then went outside, back to the before-supper drink he had been enjoying when William returned.

"I'll never get these things clean," his mother said, sounding more sorrowful than angry now, as though the world would come to an end before she had time to switch on the washing machine.

(18)

"He'll have to pay for the cleaning out of his pocket-money, that's all," his father said from the garden.

"I'll tell you one thing, mind, William," his mother said firmly, and she wagged her finger in his face. "You'd better behave yourself for the rest of this week, d'you hear? I'm not having my holiday spoilt. So think on."

William did not reply. He thought he would remember the pattern of the tiles on Miss James's cottage floor for the rest of his life. He had been concentrating on them so hard in order to keep his mind free of the storm blowing around him that they were etched deep into his memory.

His mother left him standing there, staring, went into the kitchen, took a plate of food from the oven and carried it to the table.

"There's your supper," she said. "Sit yourself down and eat it. And I don't want to hear another word out of you."

4

Miss James knocked quietly on William's bedroom door. "May I come in?" she said.

"If you want," William said. He was sitting on his bed sorting out his belongings.

"I thought I'd see that you're comfortably settled before I set off for Bristol." Miss James closed the door behind her. "Is there anything you need?"

William shook his head without looking up.

"More blankets? It can be cold in the night at this time of year."

William shook his head again. He did not know what to say. He liked Miss James, knew she was trying to be friendly. But sometimes he found talking to adults hard. Especially when they wanted him to.

Being told off before supper didn't help, either. William had left the table as soon as he dared, come to his room, changed into his old jeans, a scruffy sweater and his trekkers that had holes in the toes. At least now he could do what he liked without worrying about messing himself up. Not that there was any prospect of this anyway. He wouldn't be allowed out again that night.

"I hope you like your bedroom," Miss James was

saying. "It's still a bit bare. But I can't afford anything more plush yet."

"It's okay," William managed to say.

He had been given the choice of two bedrooms. One upstairs, across a little landing from his parents' room. The other was this one, downstairs, behind the sitting-room and next to the bathroom. He had chosen it because he would be away from his parents. He liked, too, the feeling of being on his own. And he had never slept on the ground floor anywhere before.

"This part of the cottage is new," Miss James said. "I had it built on to the old part which makes up the rest of my little house. It was a small farm once."

The room had a window that looked into the field where the crazy sheep were grazing (so William felt in good company). It had a single bed with springs that made twanging noises when you sat down. There was a small chest of drawers, painted white, and a strip of rush matting on the concrete floor. Beside the bed was a little table with a lamp standing on it made from an empty wine bottle.

That was all. Nothing on the white-painted walls —no pictures or even a mirror. William had already decided he would draw a big picture and hang it on the wall as a present for Miss James. It would be something to do during this dud holiday.

He had been thinking about what he would draw when Miss James came to see him.

"You've brought quite a lot with you I see," Miss

James was saying. "Pencils and colouring things, and paper, and books. Quite a lot."

William swallowed hard, trying to release the tightness in his throat. "Helps pass the time," he said, but his voice sounded dry and rasped.

Miss James sat on the end of his bed. He felt the mattress tip towards her.

She smiled. "Do you find it hard being an only child?" she asked, taking William by surprise with her question. "Not having brothers or sisters to play with, I mean."

"Mam says one of me is enough for anybody."

Miss James laughed. "Yes," she said. "So she's been telling me."

William forced a smile in reply.

"I'm an only child myself," Miss James said. "But I never liked it. I always wanted a brother. I can remember when I was five or maybe it was when I was six, but about then, I wanted a brother so badly I started saving milk-bottle tops."

"Milk-bottle tops?" William said, puzzled.

"Yes. Milk always came in bottles then with silver foil tops. Now it's mostly those awful greasy cartons."

"But why did you save them?"

"Because somebody told me that if I saved enough I'd get a baby brother."

William could not help laughing. "Milk-bottle tops! For a baby brother! That's crazy!"

"Maybe. But that's what I did. I saved every milk-bottle top that came into the house. I got all my mother's friends, and all our neighbours, and my aunts and grandparents and anyone else I could persuade to save theirs for me too. And once a week I went round everybody and collected them."

"But didn't you . . . *know*?" William asked.

"At five? Did you, when you were five?"

"I can't remember," William said, giggling now.

"I saved until I had eight hundred and sixty-three. I remember the number exactly because I counted them every Friday night. I always hoped that I'd have enough to get a baby brother on the Saturday, when my parents went shopping. I thought you bought baby brothers at the baby care shop, you see."

William thought his sides would split. "That's wild!"

"But every Friday my mother told me I still didn't have plenty. When I reached eight hundred and sixty-three I decided enough was enough. A baby brother wasn't worth more than that many milk-bottle tops."

"I've never heard anything so batty," William said through his giggles. He rolled on the bed to try and ease the ache in his stomach, but couldn't stop laughing.

Miss James was laughing too. "Well, I'm glad revealing my darkest secret has cheered you up," she said when William began to get control of himself. "I'm sorry you had such a bad time before supper."

William sat up, sobered by the memory.

"It's okay," he said. "I'm used to it."

Miss James stood up. "And maybe I can do something to liven up your holiday. For a start, I've just time to show you the outbuildings. You might find them useful in the next few days. Especially if it rains."

The outbuildings were a row of ramshackle cowbyres running at right-angles from the back of the cottage.

"When I've enough money," Miss James said as she led William outside, "I'm going to turn them into a flat for my friends to stay in."

She showed William one room that was used for storing logs and kindling. There was a huge tree-felling axe there with a haft as long as William was tall and a blade bigger than his two hands put together. There was a chopping block and a bow-saw with enormous shark-teeth on its blade.

Another room had a carpenter's bench in it, with a few old tools lying on it, dulled and rusting from lack of use. "I do my repairs here," Miss James said. "I'm not very good though. Repair my thumbs with the hammer mostly!"

A third room was empty, but a lot of bird-droppings covered the floor. "Owls," Miss James said, whispering, and pointing to the ceiling where there was a hole. "They live up there. Don't disturb them. You'll have fun watching them in the evenings, if you're patient and keep still."

Then she pushed open a rickety door into a fourth byre.

"This is the one for you," she said. "I call it the junk shop. I store my old rubbish here."

William stood in the doorway and looked around. Plaster had dropped off the walls in great jigsaw pieces. The floor was littered with objects piled higgledy-piggledy, some covered with dust, some freshly dumped there.

William listed the stuff off in his mind. Two bicycles, one with a crossbar one without. Five old storm lanterns, their cases rusted brown (he recognized them from pictures he had seen in books). A battered tennis racket with some strings broken. Three deck-chairs, folded and stacked against a wall. A packing-case that looked as if it was full of old camping gear. A worn tent bag with tent cloth spilling out. Something made of thick yellow plastic and lying in a crumpled pile. A valve poked out of the bundle of the kind you use when blowing something up with a hand pump. ("An inflatable dinghy," Miss James said when she saw William looking at it. "I used to have fun with it at the seaside.") A coil of rope, tangled. A pair of short-arm oars. All sorts of gardening tools. A pyramid of cardboard boxes that gave no clue to their contents. Two large inner tubes from lorry wheels. A beach football. And a huge, goofy-looking plastic duck.

William was already turning over in his mind the possibility of setting up the tent in the garden, and maybe even digging a camp fire for making barbecue meals. He had never done that before.

"Do what you like with any of it," Miss James said. "Mostly it's useless. This is going to be the bathroom in the new flat."

William could tell from the way she looked round that Miss James saw quite clearly in her imagination exactly how it was all going to be.

Heavy boots came towards them along the track.

"Anybody at home?"

"Gareth!" Miss James shouted and went outside.

The man was no taller than Miss James but looked tough and weathered. His face was red and lined. He wore an old cap, colourless with sweat and dirt, and a holey sweater with a grubby shirt-collar sticking out. His trousers were green corduroy with the cord rubbed away at the knees. His heavy boots had just come through mud. He smelt of cows and milk and a fusty warmth.

"Hello, Gareth, how are you?" Miss James said. She was obviously pleased to see him.

"Fine, now, fine. I thought I should come before you go."

"That's good of you. This is William. He's staying with his parents for a week. William, this is Mr Davies. He farms all round the cottage."

"Nice to meet you," Mr Davies said.

"Hello," William said, tongue-tied again.

"Thought there was somebody," Mr Davies said to Miss James. "When the car come up."

"Just for a week."

"I'll keep an eye then. Yes."

"Thanks. William here isn't looking forward to it though."

"No? Nice weather, plenty of country. The sea near. Nothing to do. You should love it, boy. Wish I could get some!" Mr Davies laughed.

After she had waited a moment for William to speak, Miss James said, "I think he wanted to go camping by the sea."

"It w-wasn't . . ." William began after another awkward silence while Mr Davies and Miss James smiled down at him. He wanted to say that it wasn't proper camping he liked but being by the sea in a caravan, which felt like camping but was as comfortable as home. And that he wanted to be in a caravan in the place they had always gone to where he had friends and knew about everything. But saying all that was too much.

"Camping?" Mr Davies said. "Our Gwyn is camping. Well, that's what he calls it, you know. He has a tent over by Pentyn Head. Mind you, he comes home soon as he's hungry!"

Mr Davies and Miss James laughed together.

"Best of both worlds," Miss James said. "Trust Gwyn. I thought I'd seen him out there this last few days."

"No flies on our Gwyn, that's true," Mr Davies said. "Old head on young shoulders. But he'd like a bit of company, I expect."

"What a good idea," Miss James said. "Maybe you could arrange it, Gareth?"

"I'll mention it for you, I will, with pleasure. He comes home morning and evening for the milking. He's there now finishing. I'll speak to him."

William felt weak. "I don't think . . ."

Miss James put an arm round his shoulders.

"Don't worry about your parents," she said. "I'll have a word with them. They'll agree, you'll see."

"I d-d-didn't mean . . ."

"And don't you worry about our Gwyn," Mr Davies butted in. "He'll be glad to help. Yes."

"That's settled then," Miss James said brightly. "Your holiday is looking up already, William. I told you it would." She turned towards the cottage. "Come in, Gareth," she said. "I'll introduce you to William's parents."

Miss James and Mr Davies went off inside.

William did not follow.

5

William slumped back against the outbuildings' wall, and stared, unseeing, at the grazing sheep. Not one of them looked back or even bleated. They might have been deliberately ignoring him.

A wave of homesickness swamped him. William could just feel himself back in his own room three hundred miles away, surrounded by his own things. His model airplanes, which he was busy hanging from his bedroom ceiling in a swooping squadron of all his favourites. And his gear for drawing and painting.

William wasn't terrific at drawing yet: he knew that. But he also knew somehow that one day he would be very good at it. And he enjoyed drawing and painting more than anything else he could think of. Every Saturday morning he went off in search of a new subject. Every Saturday afternoon, and sometimes most of Sunday too, he sat in his room making his latest picture. Even building his airplanes did not give him as much pleasure as the touch of pencil on paper, and the soft, flowing wetness of a paintbrush filling in colours.

His room walls were slowly being covered with pictures he had thought worth keeping. His mother complained, of course. She said they and his swooping airplanes collected dust and made the place untidy. But she never took them down, even though she sometimes threatened to when she was in a bad temper because of something William had done.

William also had his collection of books in his room. They were arranged in sections. Not sections like they have in libraries, but sections William organized according to a plan of his own. All the books he liked best were on one shelf by the side of his bed; he could reach out and pick one any time he wanted. Those he liked least were stacked on the top of his wardrobe, because he could never actually bring himself to throw a book away. Even if he did not think much of what it was about he still liked a book for itself: the cover and the paper and the way the words were printed. One of the things he wanted to find out a lot more about was printing.

Now, as he slouched against the wall, he could *feel* all that, could imagine it, like a picture he might have drawn himself. It all felt part of him, like his teeth and his arms and legs were part of him. And all that part of him that was at home seemed as though he had cut it off, had left it behind, betrayed.

He knew if he thought about it he would cry. He could feel tears swelling in his eyes, and his throat wanted to swallow too much.

He wondered desperately how to distract himself. Remembering the plastic football he had seen in the junk shop, he went in and got it.

For a while, he bounced the ball about on the track, then, because the homesickness still prickled in his mouth and eyes, he began kicking it against the outbuilding. Harder and harder.

Soon he was smashing the ball violently against the stones. And somehow he managed each shot exactly, so that the ball rebounded straight back to his feet. Usually he was poor at football. All left feet, his father said. So now he felt a bad-tempered pleasure in being able to do well something he could only do badly when he was calm and being watched.

"Nobody," he growled aloud, "listens."

He slammed the ball again. It thumped against the grey Welsh stones and flew back at him.

"Nobody . . . *ever* . . . listens."

He stopped the ball with his right foot, and aimed a vicious kick. But this time he lost balance. His foot grazed the ball, which spun away at an angle.

William turned to chase after it.

Standing in the track a few yards away and directly in the path of the spinning football was the ginger-haired boy he had met that afternoon.

The boy trapped the ball with an expert left foot.

"Who won't listen to what, English?" he said, grinning.

The anger went out of William like air from a balloon. He even sighed as it went. Suddenly, his trekkers were lead boots as heavy as a deep-sea diver's.

An age seemed to William to pass as he and the boy sized each other up.

William knew that if he wasn't careful he would have to fight. This was the kind of boy who would enjoy a battle. Afterwards he would treat you as if you were his best friend. But only afterwards. First you would have to prove yourself.

Which was all very well if you enjoyed a good fight. But William did not. It wasn't that he was a coward. At least, he didn't think he was. He believed he would stand up to anyone if ever he thought it was important to do so. But no one had ever faced him with anything *that* important.

Mostly, he got out of tricky encounters by turning the whole thing into a joke. Usually a joke against himself. But as he stared at this boy, with the longing for home still gripping his mind, he could not think of one funny thing to say. Not one.

"Doesn't surprise me nobody listens if you say nothing," the boy said at last. He started dribbling the ball back and forth across the track, slowly and very skilfully. There was a sly smile on his face and he kept looking at William, challenging him to take the ball.

"I'll tell you what," the boy said after seven or eight passes back and forth, "I'll give you a game of Shoot."

William watched, knowing the boy was good with a ball.

"How about it then?" the boy said. "Best of ten

shots." He trapped the ball with his left foot and faced William squarely. "The goal can be the edges of the road. You be goalie first."

William knew there was nothing else for it. He would have to play this game, or demand his ball back.

Crouching down, goal-keeper fashion, William stretched out his arms in front of him, hoping he looked less foolish than he felt. He was about as good at goal-keeping as a giraffe would be at tennis, and it would not take this boy five minutes to find that out.

The boy dribbled away up the track, turned, and came back, picking up speed and weaving about. William could see that in his mind the boy wasn't on a rutted cart-track at all but in the middle of a huge football stadium, storming up to score against heavy opposition.

The boy ran to within six feet of William before he let loose a beautifully timed kick that sent the ball flying straight past William's left side. William did not even see the ball slip by, it went so fast, but he heard it stotting away down the track behind him.

"Goal!" the boy shouted, jumping into the air with victory arm thrusts, just as he had seen players do after scoring on televised soccer matches. "Wales one, England nil."

William retrieved the ball and came jogging back, somehow managing to keep the ball just ahead of him with careful, gentle toe jabs. He was grateful for at least accomplishing this successfully.

The boy was still bouncing about, overdoing his

excitement. But as William came close, he crouched down, his turn now to be in goal.

"Okay, English," he shouted. "Your shot. Strike, man, strike!"

William stumbled into a kick. His aim was accurate enough, but his kick lacked power. The ball slithered unimpressively towards the boy.

"*Eeeasy!*" the boy shouted, flinging himself down in a far more dramatic save than the shot needed. "Told you," he boasted as he sprang to his feet again, grinning, the ball clutched neatly to his chest.

He turned and ran back for his second shot. As he did so, William heard the cottage door open, letting out voices all talking at once.

"Well now, look you here," he heard Mr Davies say. He was coming towards William with Miss James and his parents behind. "Your William and our Gwyn has got together already."

William straightened up as if Mr Davies had slapped him hard on the back.

At that moment the ball flew past him again.

"Goal!" bellowed Gwyn jumping about even more wildly than before. "Wales two, England nil."

Mr Davies scooped up the ball in a thick, dinner-plate hand. "Likes his soccer does our Gwyn," he said. "Bit of a heretic, when you think about it, a Welshman liking soccer more than rugby."

Miss James smiled. "I knew they'd like each other," she said. "Trust kids to make friends while the grown-ups are still talking about it."

"Never slow coming forward, our Gwyn," Mr Davies said.

"Unlike some we could mention," William's father said.

William glared at him.

"Hello, Gwyn," Miss James said. "You seem to be winning."

Gwyn grinned triumphantly.

"Come you here, will you, boy," Mr Davies said.

Gwyn went to his father but he was eyeing William's parents, not making any effort to disguise that he was weighing them up.

"Their William here wants to do a bit of camping, see," Mr Davies said quietly to Gwyn. (Just as if we weren't listening, William thought.) "I said you might have him with you, eh?"

Gwyn's face clouded. "Oh, Da!" he said.

Mr Davies took him by the shoulder. "Remember that calf now. Yes? I'll help you there, if you'll help me with this. All right?"

Gwyn hung his head. "I don't know."

"Don't force him, if he doesn't want to, Mr Davies," William's mother said.

"Don't you worry," Mr Davies said without taking his eyes from Gwyn. "He might not be slow coming forward, our Gwyn, but he hates changing plans. He'll be all right when he's used to the idea, won't you, boy?"

Gwyn muttered something in Welsh; Mr Davies replied sharply, wagging a finger at him.

There was silence. Larks sang in the setting sun. Sheep bleated. Insects whined by like self-propelled bullets.

"Okay," Gwyn said at last. "He can come if he wants." But he did not sound enthusiastic.

William stood aghast. He tried desperately to think how to stop what was going on. It was like a nightmare in which he was trying to run away from something dreadful, but no matter how hard he tried he couldn't move. His feet were glued to the spot.

But suddenly anger put words into his head and he blurted them out.

"I don't want to come with you anyway."

William saw his father stiffen. "Don't be so rude," he snapped. "Mr Davies and Gwyn are putting themselves out for you. At least show some gratitude."

"I don't want to camp with him," William said defiantly.

"You've talked of nothing else all the way here but camping by the sea," his mother said. "Now you turn your nose up when it's offered. I can't understand you, William."

"I didn't m-mean that kind of c-camping."

"I don't think you know what you mean."

Miss James said, "I expect he's tired. He's had a long day. Tomorrow things will look different."

"You're right, Miss James," William's father said. "Come on, young man. Let's be having you. Bed. Long past your time anyway."

"Our Gwyn will be over tomorrow morning," Mr Davies said. "They can sort it out between them."

"That's it," William's father said. "They're old enough to take care of themselves. I don't know what we're trying so hard for."

The adults laughed. William's father took William firmly by the shoulder and steered him towards the cottage door. There would be no sympathy, William could tell from the hardness of his father's grip.

"Thanks for your help, Mr Davies," his father called. "We'll see you in the morning, Gwyn."

6

"How about it, English?" Gwyn said. "We'll have a pact."

"Stop calling me English," William said.

"That's what you are, isn't it, boy?"

"You wouldn't like it if I called you Taffy."

Gwyn laughed. "Sticks and stones."

"Or Coppernob."

"Okay, okay!" Gwyn held his hand out with two fingers crossed. "Barley."

"We say skinch up our way."

"Skinch, then."

William looked up at Gwyn, making sure he meant it. But he couldn't tell. Gwyn had the kind of eyes that could hide whatever he was thinking. "All right. Barley." He held out two crossed fingers.

Gwyn squatted on the ground beside William, leaning his back against the garden wall.

William had been there half an hour already, shaded by the wall from the early morning sun. He was drawing a sketch of the cottage on a large sheet of paper.

Gwyn bent across him to give the drawing a close inspection.

"Pretty good at that, you are," he said.

"Not bad," William said, pushing Gwyn away.

"Better than at football I'd think."

"You're not wrong about that, either," William said, pretending unconcern but feeling the sting.

"Better than at climbing trees as well, boyo." Gwyn chuckled. "Going by what I saw yesterday, anyway."

"We can't all be King Kong, like you," William said.

"Fighting talk that," Gwyn said. "There's brave!"

William went on working with his pencil, refusing to be roused.

He had been woken early by sheep chomping grass outside his window. He'd never thought grazing animals could make so much noise just chewing.

His father was already up; William could hear him in the bathroom. He knew his father would be getting ready to go fishing.

William would like to have gone with him. But his father got bad-tempered if William did anything that might disturb the fish, or if he handled his rod wrongly, or even if he asked questions.

Then, as well, his father fished for hours on end; he never stopped, not even for food. He just fished and fished, all day long. William got bored to the point of collapse long before his father was ready to go home.

All in all, it was better if William did not go. But that always turned out to be wrong too. For some reason William could not understand, his father then thought he was being unfriendly and got sulky about it.

William sighed. They called this a holiday!

The morning was overcast and cool. He dressed, made himself some bread and marmalade, cleared away his own and his father's breakfast things. By then the sun had broken through, so he went out and began his drawing.

A few minutes after he settled down, his mother took a bleary-eyed look at the weather, said, "Drawing again? You'd be better off fishing with your dad," and went back inside, her slippers flapping on the tiles.

William knew she would have breakfast, then lie on a beach mattress on her bedroom floor, where she could read a book while the sun-ray lamp deepened her tan. He'd see no more of her that morning, and heaven help him if he bothered her.

"You do a lot of that drawing?" Gwyn said after a while.

William nodded. "It's my best thing."

"You could draw me, eh?" Gwyn said, laughing. "Do my portrait, like posh people."

William looked at him. "I've never done a person before. It would be hard."

"Always a first time, eh, English?"

William sighed.

"Sorry, boy, forgot. I know, I'll call you Picasso."

"I don't like that either."

"Fussy. But what about my picture?"

"Maybe. Later on. When I've heard about this pact."

Gwyn shifted position so that he could look William straight in the face.

"It's like this," he said. "You don't want to go camping with me. That's what you said last night."

"You don't want to have me, either."

"Well, it isn't quite like that, boy."

"*William.*"

"I'll settle for Bill. How's that?"

"All right. Get on."

"Mind, I think Picasso is best."

William stuffed his drawing between the pages of the book he was resting on, and put it aside. He couldn't draw properly with this chatter going on. "Look," he said. "Stop blathering about my name, will you! If you want to talk about this pact . . ."

"I do, Billy, I do," Gwyn said. "I was telling you." He plucked a stalk of grass and began sucking it. "It's not easy."

"What's difficult?" William said. "You don't want to take me camping and I don't want to go with you."

"Ah . . . but . . ." Gwyn said. "There's the calf, you see."

"No, I don't see."

"I got two already. I'm building my own herd like."

"You mean," William said, "you *own* two cows?"

"I do. I work for my dad, see. He pays me. I save what he pays. When there's enough I buy a calf."

"Why do you do that?"

"When the time comes right, I'll sell. Make a profit. Buy more calves with the profit. Like that, you see."

William had never heard of anyone his own age actually owning anything as valuable as cows and even buying and selling them. The idea intrigued him, put his drawing into the shade. Somehow it also made him feel childish and ordinary. But that did not quell his interest.

"That's smashing!" he said.

Gwyn took the compliment without a sign of pleasure. "It's all right," he said. "But only a start, boy. And that's the thing, you see."

"What's the thing?" William said, eager to know.

"If you come camping, my dad says he'll give me a bit more towards another calf."

"More?"

"Money, of course. And he'll take me to market next week. Let me bid for a good beast."

William's excitement evaporated; he could see where Gwyn was leading him. "And if I don't?"

"That's right. He won't."

William stared coldly at Gwyn, who stared back unblinking.

"Why should your father do something like that?" William said.

"Miss James asked him about you and me camping. My dad and Miss James is friends. She bought the cottage off him, see. And she pays my dad to look after it when she isn't here and there's visitors. Like you. So my dad, he doesn't want to let her down. That's how it is."

William was having to battle with himself to stay calm. "And you want me to come camping so you can earn some lousy money to buy calves with!"

Gwyn looked puzzled; he said, "What's so wrong with that? It's a fair trade. I want a calf. You want a week's camping. I give you a week and get a calf for it. You don't have to pay a penny. Sounds a pretty good bargain to me, boyo."

"*William!*" He stood up, furious. "I d-don't want to c-camp," he shouted.

Gwyn pushed himself to his feet and stood like a snappy sheepdog facing a wayward sheep.

"Then what did you go on about camping for?" he barked. "Getting everybody churned up."

"I didn't!" William felt he was bleating. "I said I w-w-wanted to have a holiday in a c-caravan by the sea. Like we always do. That's *like* camping but it's b-b-better."

Gwyn growled at him and turned away, hands dug into pockets, face snarling at the ground.

"You could have said. Stopped everybody pestering me. Raising hopes."

He kicked toe holes in the grass.

The way Gwyn was behaving made William feel he had committed a crime. He knew this was foolish, but he couldn't help himself. Sometimes he thought he must be going daft, because whenever anyone talked about a crime, or something going wrong, he always felt guilty. Even if he had been nowhere near what had happened and had only just heard about it. He would blush, his toes would squirm in his shoes, his eyes would refuse to look anyone in the face.

He was acting like that now, quite against his will. Yet none of this was his fault. If his mother hadn't talked to Miss James . . . and if Miss James hadn't talked to Mr Davies . . . if the adults had all just minded their own business . . .

"I tried," he said, wanting to explain, but at the same time wondering why he should. Gwyn, after all, was as bad as the adults. He was just wanting to use William to get himself another calf. But William couldn't stop himself. He wanted Gwyn to understand. Wanted to be friends if he could. He had to go on, though inside he was kicking himself for it. "I tried. But they wouldn't listen. My mother and dad just want to get on with their holiday. They don't want me in their way. So they didn't listen. You don't know my dad . . ."

"And you don't know mine," Gwyn said. "If you don't come camping with me now, he'll say I put you off. Then I'll have a terrible time, boy, I tell you. Terrible. For a month."

"Rats!" William said. "All you want is the stinking money for a rotten calf."

Gwyn spluttered something in Welsh and flung

himself on to the ground. He was almost at bursting point.

William leaned against the garden wall. Whatever he did, he was in a pickle. No doubt about that. If he did not go camping he would be grumbled at whenever he was found skulking about the house at a loose end. Worse still, if he asked to be taken to the sea, there would be ructions.

All things considered, he thought, maybe it would be best if he let Gwyn take him camping. That would be better than mooching about the cottage and being told off. And maybe Gwyn would show him his cows. William couldn't help being interested in them. He had never been on a farm before and among cows and horses and pigs, not to mention the farm machinery.

He was slowly working himself into a mood to make peace when Gwyn said very quietly: "Tell you what. I got a secret. Special. I'll show you. Then maybe you'll want to camp."

William said nothing for a moment. He still did not trust Gwyn; but his curiosity was roused. No reason to be hasty, though.

"What is it, this special thing?" he asked, coolly.

Gwyn sat up, cross-legged. "Don't know if I should show you till you swear not to tell anybody else," he said. He was almost whispering. "It's why I didn't want you camping with me, see."

William pretended loss of interest. "I don't see," he said flatly.

Gwyn sighed. Just mentioning his secret was costing him dearly. William was glad to have the upper hand for once.

"This camping," Gwyn muttered. "It's just a blind. I'm not that keen. Not just a couple of fields from home, you see. But from my camp I can keep an eye on . . . this thing. And nobody asks no questions about what I'm up to. My dad nor nobody." He paused, then said with a wink, "I got plans for it."

"Plans!" William said, mocking. "You're all plans." But he was straining to know Gwyn's secret. "All right. I'll tell you what. You show me your secret. If it's worth it, I'll camp with you."

Gwyn's perky manner revived. "Okay, Picasso," he said, standing up. "But, you have to swear to keep my secret. No matter what."

William laughed for the first time in twelve hours. "You're on," he said.

"Put your hand out," Gwyn ordered.

William held out his right hand. Gwyn took it and gripped it firmly.

"You swear," he said in solemn tones, "to keep my secret and tell nobody ever till I say you can. Swear."

"I swear," William said, suddenly feeling solemn too.

"Straight?"

"Straight."

"Cut your throat and hope to die?"

"Cut my throat and hope to die."

"Spit to the left. Spit to the right."

William obeyed.

"You're sworn," Gwyn said, releasing William's hand. Without a pause, he turned on his heel and jogged off down the track.

"Come on, Picasso," he said over his shoulder. "I'll show you my secret."

7

Gwyn said nothing as they trudged across the fields. He walked with the confidence of someone who knows exactly where he is, hardly ever looking up from the ground.

William plodded along behind. He had not yet seen the sea and kept straining for a first glimpse of that straight line of horizon that marks the joining of sea and sky. On a day like this, with a heat haze in the air, it might be difficult to make out.

But already there was the tangy smell of the seashore reaching him across the grass. He began to feel excited about the prospect of being at the water's edge. This was what he liked most: the meeting of land and sea, with the waves washing up and back.

Long ago William had decided that when he was old enough to do what he pleased, he would live by the sea in a house with an uninterrupted view all along the shore. Maybe, he thought now, he might become an artist and then he would be able to work as well as live in his house. His studio would be the room with the best view, so that he could watch the sea in all its moods while he worked.

He looked at Gwyn's sturdy body walking ahead

of him. "Do you have to look after your calves all by yourself?" he called.

"I do," Gwyn said without slowing his pace or looking back. "Who else would do it?"

"Doesn't your dad help?"

"Not him! He told me that when I started. If I want cows I have to rear them myself."

"But what if one of them is ill?"

"I get the vet, stupid. The forms is worst."

"The forms?"

"From the government. You have to fill in questions. I'm no good at writing. They're a prying lot, the government."

"Doesn't your dad help with them?"

Gwyn laughed. "No, no. He's worse than me. He writes I DO NOT WISH TO JOIN across them in Welsh and sends them back."

"Doesn't that get him into trouble?"

"Not much. They come and see him, English men in suits, you know. But Da acts thick in the head and not able to speak English and they go away after a bit."

They had come to a rise in the field. William could hear beyond it the sound of waves on the shore.

Together he and Gwyn ran to the top, where, to William's surprise and pleasure, the field ended abruptly in a sharp edge. A steep bank scurried down from their feet, all boulders and loose rocks and slithering soil, to a pebbly beach. And the sea.

There were no great rolling waves today. The surface was calm, undulating in long serpent swells that finished in a surge of froth, sucking in and out, pushing sand and pebbles and seaweed and jetsam back and forth.

To his right, just in sight beyond a bluff of headland, William could see a little island standing off from the shore. It rose from the sea like a pyramid with a flat top. Its steep cliffs were made of grey rock rising up in jagged steps full of crevices. But the top was green, like a soft cushion on a stool.

William took a deep breath, swung his eyes round the sea-view, and smiled at Gwyn.

Gwyn smiled back, his eyes shining too, and William knew Gwyn liked the sight and sound of sea and shore as much as he did himself. For the first time since they had met, William thought he might like Gwyn.

"Down here," Gwyn said.

Immediately he plunged over the bank side, arms flapping to keep his balance, his feet stomping and sliding and pumping like pistons. His spiky ginger hair bounced at each thump of his feet, and he yodelled a charging cry.

William laughed at the reckless figure, and picked his way more carefully down the treacherous bank.

At the bottom long before him, Gwyn waited, lounging on a great grey-blue boulder as if he had been there all day.

"Show off," William said, as he caught up.

"Easy, boyo," Gwyn said.

"When you know it like you do."

Gwyn grinned agreement. They set off along the beach towards the bluff.

The pebbly beach made walking difficult. The smooth little stones slipped about when William stood on them and he had to watch his balance. So they edged towards the sea where a strip of sand, still glistening wet from the retreating waves, would make an easier path.

"Take your shoes and socks off," Gwyn said when they reached the sand. "We'll have to in a minute anyway."

William tugged off his trekkers, tied them together with the laces, stuffed his socks inside, and slung the shoes round his neck. Now he felt more at home: every year this was just what he did when he went exploring the beach from the caravan at their usual holiday place.

Gwyn stood up, barefooted, his shoes stuffed inside his shirt. "Race you!" he said and set off at a gallop along the beach, deliberately running in and out of the water, his feet sending spray flying.

With his longer legs William had no trouble overtaking. As he came near, Gwyn suddenly turned sideways and began kicking water up at him. William kicked back. A running battle started with sand and water for weapons. Neither took much trouble to avoid being splashed. Soon they were giggling at the madness of it all.

Then, after an especially energetic kick, William's trekkers went flying from his neck. He dived and caught them. Gwyn made a grab at them too, but tripped and fell.

Instead of jumping up at once, as William expected, Gwyn lay where he had fallen. Instinctively, William reached to help him. Too late he saw Gwyn was shamming. Before he could dodge away, Gwyn's hand shot out, grabbing his ankle. Before he could do anything to save himself, William was lying at Gwyn's side in the surging tide.

"English fool!" Gwyn said through his laughter.

"Welsh yob!"

Their giggles became uncontrollable. They rolled against each other, clung on to each other's arms and bodies, tumbled about in the sea.

In seconds they were soaked to the skin. Their clothes, sopping, stuck to them. Each time a wave broke over their faces, they spluttered, pretending to be drowning men; when the wave swept out they flapped about like stranded fish.

When they were out of breath and had had enough, they hauled themselves on to a huge flat boulder poking up from the beach above the tide line, and lay panting together, side by side on their backs.

"You're bonkers, you know that, Picasso," Gwyn said, when they were calm again.

"You aren't so sane yourself, cowboy," William said. "But what about this secret?"

"Ready when you are," Gwyn said.

They set off again. His still damp clothes made William feel cold inside.

As they rounded the bluff, William saw it hid a kind of inlet, like a huge bite out of the cliff, which rose up, not in a bank, but into an overhanging precipice.

The little island would have fitted neatly into the bite. Perhaps, William thought, it had broken free and drifted out to sea one day long ago, and got stuck half a mile away.

At the end of the inlet, at sea level, William made out the dark opening of a cave.

"In there," Gwyn said, pointing. The sea washed all round it and right up to the cliff for quite a stretch on either side.

"How do we get there?" he asked.

"The sea looks deeper than it is," Gwyn said. "It's nearly low tide. We can wade. Any other time it's dangerous. From about half tide up to full, we'd have to swim."

William shivered. Not from fear, he hoped, but from the clammy dampness of his clothes. "It looks pretty dangerous now," he said. There was white fume where the sea hit the cliff face.

"Stick close to me, boy," Gwyn said in that boastful tone William disliked.

Step by step for twenty paces the water rose higher and higher up William's legs, till it was round his knees and up to the middle of Gwyn's thighs.

"Does it get any deeper?" he called anxiously.

"A few inches," Gwyn called back. "But the tide is going out still."

By the time they were half way across, Gwyn was wading waist high and William was up to his hips. What if Gwyn put his foot into a hole, William wondered, or stumbled on a hidden rock? What if he did himself?

The thought brought him out in goose-flesh and a cold sweat. He remembered his father teaching him to swim a couple of years ago. At first his father had been gentle and helpful, keeping hold of William and giving him confidence. But then, suddenly, he had stepped away just as William launched himself in a deep place.

William had sunk under the surface, swallowing mouthfuls of water. When he came up, panicking and thrashing his arms, he saw through his water-logged eyes his father laughing and not moving to rescue him. He hated the memory and shook his head to get rid of it.

William gritted his teeth and ploughed on behind Gwyn. Underwater currents swirled strongly round his legs, and the rise and fall of passing waves made him think each time that they would topple him off his feet.

About twenty paces from the cave entrance the ground began to slope up steeply. With a relieved spurt, they strode out of the water and stood together on dry land, the cave mouth gaping darkly in front of them.

"Now listen," Gwyn said, full of seriousness. "We have to be quiet now. I don't want to scare it. Okay?"

William nodded, trembling from cold and excitement.

Gwyn eyed him. "Don't forget, Billy-Will. You swore not to tell. Not nobody. Ever."

"I know, I know," William said through locked teeth. "Get on. I'm perishing."

Indian fashion, Gwyn leading the way, they stalked into the cave.

8

Inside, the cave was not as deep as William expected. Really it was just a huge, spoon-shaped hole in the rock. But it echoed eerily the sound of the sea and the cries of gulls flying by outside.

The sandy floor was littered with boulders, rocks and pebbles. Gwyn picked a way through them. After a few yards he held out his arm, bringing William to a halt. Then he pointed to the back corner of the cave across from where they stood.

William squinted into the unusual light: gloomy, yet somehow bright too from sunlight reflected off the sea. At first he could pick out nothing but rocks.

Then one of the rocks moved.

"What is it?" he asked.

"Won't hurt," Gwyn said, "so long as you keep away from the business end."

They went nearer. William made out what seemed like a fat black sausage about three feet long, lying on a nest of white stuff. As he came close, one end of the sausage lifted up and let out a hissing snarl.

"Seal pup," Gwyn said, stopping six feet away.

Now William could clearly see a soft dog-like head, with fine whiskers fanning from its nose. No ears were visible but the eyes were large, chestnut brown, and sorrowful. Tears made a wet patch of fur under them as the pup stared up at him.

"It's crying!" he said, feeling he wanted to stroke the poor animal and comfort it.

"They always do," Gwyn said. "Dunno why. Daft, isn't it?"

"How did it get here?"

"Born here," Gwyn said. "I saw it happen." He could not disguise his pride.

"You saw it!" William said, envious. "Great! Was it . . ." He did not know how to say what he meant.

"About three weeks back," Gwyn said. "Just like our bitch having pups."

William did not dare tell Gwyn he had never seen a dog having pups. In fact, he had never seen any animal giving birth. Except in biology films at school, of course, and he knew that was not at all the same. "I wish I'd been here," he said.

"I couldn't get too close," Gwyn said. "They scare easy, see. Seals desert their young if they know there's people about."

William looked round anxiously. "Where's the mother now?"

"Gone."

"You mean we've scared her off?"

"No, she went last week. The pup is born, see, and the mother feeds it for about two weeks. After that she never comes back."

"What she do that for?" William said, indignant. "No wonder the poor thing is crying all the time."

Gwyn laughed. "Idiot. It's not crying because of that!"

"What then?"

"I dunno. But it's not that. They all do it. The mother did it as well."

Gwyn started picking up large rocks and lugging them to within ten feet of the seal, where he set them down, one on another. William paid no attention, his eyes fixed on the pup. He found the animal fascinating, wanted to know all about it, wanted to touch it, wanted to watch everything it did.

"Why doesn't the mother take the pup with her, though?" The parent seal's heartlessness puzzled him.

Gwyn said, "A fisherman down Pentyn told me seals suckle their pups for two weeks then go back to sea. He says pups don't really like the sea. So they stay where the mother leaves them, living off their body fat. He says it's only hunger that drives them into the water in the end. They have to swim to get food. It's all instinct, you see."

"So this one has been all by itself for a week now and is slowly starving." William went a step nearer the pup and squatted on his haunches to take a closer look.

The velvet-covered bundle of fat shuffled on its front flipper-paws, raised its head and let out a noise that was half dog-snarl and half cat-hiss.

(58)

"They got a nasty bite," Gwyn said. He was still busy piling rocks in a row behind William.

"Their fur looks lovely," William said, admiring the sleek blackness.

"You can stroke it if you keep behind the head."

William edged forwards. The seal tried to swivel so that it could face him, but was either too heavy for its own strength or its flippers could not get enough grip on the sand.

His heart pounding at the excitement, William cautiously put out his hand and touched the pup's back. To his surprise, the fur was not soft and fine as it looked, but coarse and stiff. It reminded him of the fur on a terrier dog.

At his touch, the pup tried harder than ever to twist and bite him. But its blubbery body, with thick rolls of flesh round the neck, prevented it from turning its head round far. All it could do was bleat and hiss and snarl while its eyes wept profuse tears.

William retreated a step or two. He hated causing the pup anxiety. "You're all right," he said soothingly. "There's nothing to be afraid of. I'm not going to hurt you." Without taking his eyes off the seal, he called to Gwyn, "What's that white stuff it's lying on?"

"Fur off itself," Gwyn said, busy with rocks. "When they're born they're white. After a bit, they moult. That one's just finished."

"Makes a nice bed."

"They're pretty when they're born. I expect that's why people like having coats made of their skins."

"That's cruel," William said. He had seen television news pictures of seal pups being killed. He had not liked watching.

"No different from killing lambs for meat, or cows come to that. You don't call that cruel, Billy-Will."

William turned to face Gwyn, ready to take up the argument. Instead his eyes caught sight of the rocks piled two feet high, starting at the cave wall and curving round the seal to meet the wall again.

"What's that for?" he asked.

"Ah!" Gwyn said, mysteriously. "Part of my plan, see."

"It's a wall."

"The boy's a genius!"

"But why?"

"To keep the seal in, bone-head."

9

William gaped at Gwyn, stunned.

"You're not going to try and keep it forever ...?" he managed to say loudly enough for Gwyn to hear above the echoing sea and the cries of the pup.

Gwyn placed another rock, then came and stood by William.

"I'm going to teach it tricks, see. For a start anyway. For fun. But I've a better plan than that, Picasso."

William stared at Gwyn, unbelieving, hardly daring to ask the next question. He knew what the reply would be. The answer lay like a stone in his stomach, weighing him down, and crushing the excitement of seeing the seal.

He took a couple of stumbling steps forward so that he was outside Gwyn's quickly closing wall, and sat on a knee-high boulder.

Everything around him was all at once unpleasant. The air in the cave was cold, chilling. His clothes were cloying, sticky with damp salt water. His body felt weak and tired. Especially his legs. He looked at his legs, sculptured by his clinging jeans, to make sure they were not as match-stick thin as they felt. But they were.

"Want to know the rest of my plan?" Gwyn asked.

William could say nothing. His mouth might have been paralysed. He sat rigidly still.

Gwyn said, "I'm going to start a seal farm."

William let out a long sigh. His body slumped.

Gwyn stood looking across the wall at the seal, like a farmer admiring a new addition to his herd.

"With the shortage of food in the world," he went on, "I reckon seals would be a good bet. My da is always going on about food and how there's too many people. He says that's why farming is a good job. Plenty of future in it, see. So I thought, nobody farms seals, and we've plenty round here. We could make special pens on the beach. There'd be meat, you see, and skins for fur coats as well. Good profit. Can't go wrong, man. And I could be first."

Gwyn was so excited, talking so fast, it was hard to sort out the words because of his accent.

William forced himself to look at Gwyn. "But you c-c-can't!" he said.

"Why not? We farm cows and sheep and hens and pigs and all sorts. There's even people farm fish, my da says. So why not seals?"

"I don't know," William said desperately. "It just wouldn't be . . . right . . ."

"What's wrong with it? You tell me, genius."

There was angry spite in Gwyn's voice now. He never liked being opposed.

"That seal," William said, trying hard to sort out what he really did think, and to stay calm in the face of Gwyn's rage, "that seal . . . it's wild. It's not like a pet . . . not like a dog . . . and it's not like a farm animal. It shouldn't be penned in. It's wild . . ."

"Rubbish!" Gwyn exploded. His face flushed bright red. His body stiffened. "Everything was wild once. You have to start somewhere."

William pushed himself to his feet and went to the wall. The pup turned its sorrowful eyes on him.

"But it's cruel," William said, almost pleading now. "You wouldn't be able to look after it properly. You d-d-don't know how."

"I can find out can't I? If it doesn't work I can always let the pup go," Gwyn said. "Anyway, what do you know about it? You're a city kid. A soft city kid. You don't know nothing about animals."

At that moment something inside William snapped. His desperation turned to anger. He rounded on Gwyn and shouted, "It'll be too late then." His voice echoed among the sea-birds' cries. "It'll be too weak to look after itself. Or it won't know how to swim and it'll be too late to learn."

He was looking for any argument that might help. But Gwyn's burning face and fierce eyes showed he was only getting more and more annoyed.

"It could die," William blurted out finally.

"It won't!" Gwyn yelled back. "I won't let it."

He scuttled away, picked up another rock, scampered back, piled it on to the wall. "I don't care what you say, English. That seal is mine. I'm keeping it. And I'll do what I want with it."

William shook with anger. With fear too. Fear at what he must say and do. He took a deep breath, gathering himself together.

"No." He spoke firmly and without stammering, despite his churning insides. "No, you won't."

Slowly Gwyn came from the wall, fists clenched, and stood squared up close to William. "Oh?" he said with cool menace. "And who's going to stop me?"

William braced himself.

"I am," he heard himself say, as though someone else were speaking the words.

Gwyn glowered. "You!" he said. "You couldn't knock the skin off a rice pudding."

"Think what you like," William said, "but I'm not letting you keep that seal."

Gwyn's fist smashed into William's nose.

The force of the blow sent him staggering back. His feet hit a rock, he tripped, and went sprawling to the ground.

Before he could pick himself up, stones were hitting him hard on the body.

Gwyn was shouting, "You get out of here, English rubbish! You hear? Scat! Leave my seal alone!"

Stumbling, dabbing at his bleeding nose, scrambling through the litter of rocks, William fled out of the cave, stones hailing after him.

He was in the sea up to his knees before he was out of Gwyn's range. He stopped and turned. He could hardly see for tears of pain swamping his eyes. Whenever he sniffed, he tasted the iron flavour of blood.

Gwyn was standing at the entrance of the cave like a guard before a fortress gate. "And don't forget," he shouted, anger still strident in his voice. "You swore, boy. You took an oath. You tell and I'll sort you out, see."

There was nothing to be done. William plodged slowly away towards the beach. The tide had gone down farther; the walk to shore was easier than the walk to the cave.

But he hardly noticed anyway. His mind tumbled with anger and humiliation.

"He's a fool!" William said aloud. "An idiot! His brains are pickled."

He bent as he waded to splash water on to his face. Salt stung in his wounded nose. A trace of blood swirled away on the tide.

When he reached the shore, he looked back at the cave. Gwyn was still standing there, watching, a small, almost invisible figure from this distance.

"I'm going to get that seal out of there, Gwyn Davies," William shouted. He picked up a pebble and hurled it with all his force into the sea. "I'm going to rescue that seal, I don't care what you do to stop me."

10

William sat on the bed in his room, drawing. But he wasn't paying much attention because he could not stop his mind going over and over what had happened in the cave.

He had run home fast. Luckily, his mother was out. She had left a note on the dining-room table:

GONE FOR WALK. KEEP OFF THE BISCUITS

William had washed his face to get rid of the blood sticking around his nose and to cool his anger. Refreshed a little, he changed out of his salty clothes and put on his second-best jeans and his favourite tee shirt. If his mother asked about his discarded clothes he would tell her he had fallen into a rock pool while playing on the beach.

For an hour since he got back he had been trying to calm himself with his drawing. But it wasn't working. All the time his mind kept going back to the seal pup penned behind that wall of rocks, and to his fight with Gwyn.

He gave up, threw aside his pencil and paper, and lay back on his bed, staring up at the smooth blank whiteness of the ceiling.

Back at home when he lay on his bed he could see

pictures. Pictures he had drawn and painted and stuck on the ceiling with Blu-Tack so that his mother would not grumble at pin holes. Whenever he was feeling low William would lie on his bed and look up at his pictures, and somehow they always made him feel better. He had made them. They had given him pleasure. They were proof that he could do something he was proud of, and that he could be happy.

He closed his eyes and willed himself to see in his mind's eye his own ceiling and his pictures stuck on it. One of the pictures was a special favourite. He saw it now. And realized with a tingle of excitement that it told him about the seal and why he felt so strongly about rescuing it from Gwyn.

It had happened last year. One day at school his teacher, Mrs Ainsley, had read out a poem about a dancing bear. The poet told how his mother, when she was a child, had seen this huge bear. A man had chained the bear's feet and its front paws, and took it round from place to place, showing it off to crowds of people.

He made the bear perform tricks. He made it dance, and do the roly-poly and the somersault. And when the bear had finished its tricks, the man went round with a begging cup for people to put money into.

William could imagine the whole scene. He saw the crowds laughing and cheering. He saw the man, with a stick in his hand, forcing the bear to perform tricks. Most vividly of all he saw the bear, huge and frightening. But sad too, because of the chains and because it was being made to do silly antics just to amuse people.

William could remember exactly the last lines of the poem. He said them over to himself:

> *They paid a penny for the dance,*
> *But what they saw was not the show;*
> *Only, in bruin's aching eyes,*
> *Far distant forests, and the snow.*

William had liked the poem so much he borrowed Mrs Ainsley's book and wrote the poem out carefully. Later, at home, he drew a picture of the bear. Then he stuck the poem and the drawing side by side on his bedroom ceiling.

As he lay on his bed remembering all this now, William knew that the look in the seal pup's sad and weeping eyes was what had made him realize how wrong Gwyn's plan was.

But how to save the pup? That was the problem. Gwyn wasn't going to listen to reason. And he wasn't going to stand by and let William walk into the cave and pull down the wall, and leave the pup alone. Not without putting up a fight he wasn't. And William was not going to fight. Not that way.

Was that cowardice? Maybe he really was a coward. Maybe Gwyn was right.

William turned on to his side and stared out of the window at the grazing sheep. He was struck then by the thought that he would only be a coward if he let

Gwyn get away with something as wrong as he planned.

It wasn't the way you fought that proved whether or not you were a coward, but whether you stood out against the things that were bad. And there were other ways of fighting than by battering people about.

"I don't care what you think," he said aloud, as though Gwyn could hear him across two fields and half a mile of beach and sea. "I'll fight you my own way."

He got up and went into the kitchen. He felt hungry and thirsty now, as if all this thinking had been such hard work he needed food and drink. He poured himself a glass of milk and searched for the chocolate biscuits. His mother would have hidden them. Usually she chose high places, thinking either William would not see them or would not be able to reach. This time, however, he found them inside the bread bin. He hated bread; his mother must have thought he would never look in there. He took six biscuits, stowed the rest where he had found them, drank down his milk in one quaff, and went outside.

What he needed, he decided, was a quiet place to sit and think. Somewhere his mother wouldn't look for him when she returned. The garden was too exposed—not only his mother but Gwyn might find him there if he came snooping. Then he remembered the junk shop.

He pushed open the rickety door, shoved it shut after him, and sat on one of the packing-cases in the dusty half-light. While he settled to the task of planning a rescue for the seal pup, he nibbled at his store of biscuits. Like a mouse in its den, he thought, smiling to himself.

An hour and a half later, William heard his mother calling from the cottage door.

"Will-iam . . . Where are you? Dinner."

He pulled open the junk shop door and called, "Coming."

He was ready for his meal. The biscuits had gone without his noticing, so deeply had he plunged into his thoughts as a plan grew. Already he had started preparing the equipment he needed. The junk shop had proved just the right place for a planning room; it was full of the sort of gear he wanted. In fact, it was from staring at all the junk that he had first got the idea for the rescue.

After dinner, he would have to be careful what he did. If his mother got suspicious and wanted to know what he was up to, everything would be ruined.

"Where ever have you been?" his mother asked when William came into the cottage.

"Nowhere," he said.

His mother looked him up and down.

"You've changed." It was almost an accusation.

"I fell into a pool on the beach."

"More washing! You're a nuisance, you are. It'll

have to wait." She put a plate of food on the table at William's place. "And you didn't say you were going to the beach. How many times do I have to tell you that I want to know where you are?"

"I was with Gwyn."

His mother sniffed. "Glad you've found somebody to occupy yourself with." She sat at the table, picked up her book and began reading. "At least he seems a sensible lad. Which is more than I can say for some."

His mother gave William a sharp glance over the top of her book. But he could see from her eyes that she was smiling, so she must be in a better mood.

William said, straight-faced, "We're having a great time."

"Told you," his mother said.

William dug into his beans on toast, eating as fast as he could. He wanted to be out of the way before his father returned from his fishing. His father's questions about how he had spent the day would be much more probing than his mother's. He wanted to avoid a cross-examination. And there were some details about his plan he still had to sort out in his mind.

Never before, he thought as he ate, had he ever done anything as difficult as this was going to be. Or as dangerous. And he had never ever done anything as important without his parents knowing. In fact, he realized, he did almost nothing whatever without his parents deciding for him whether or not he ought to do it. And having decided, they always told him how it should be done and how it should not.

For the first time in his whole life he would be on his own. Free to make his own decisions. He had to be. There was no other way but to do this by himself, and in his own way. Without any help from anyone.

He did not dare think what would happen if anything went wrong. There would be the biggest, most awful telling-off anyone had ever had. His parents would probably lock him up for a week.

William gulped down the last of his Coke and pushed the idea from his head. Thinking of consequences only made it harder to do what had to be done. He had to think only of his plan and carrying it out well.

He collected together his used plates and cutlery, put them quietly into the sink, and went back to the junk shop. He longed for the next few hours to be gone. He hated waiting for anything. But now—he counted them off in his head—he had to wait for over sixteen hours before he could set off for the cave.

11

Next morning the sun rose at five twenty-three. William saw it happen. By then he was already approaching the cliff edge, where the meadow plunged into the beach.

He was panting, and having to stop every few paces to catch his breath and regain his strength. The bundle he was carrying seemed five times heavier than when he had tied it up in the junk shop yesterday afternoon.

Maybe, he thought, lying awake all night had left him tired and weak. He had not dared let himself sleep in case he did not wake in time. So all night long, he had forced himself to stay awake, which had taken all his concentration and willpower. Once or twice he had dozed off, but luckily some part of his mind realized he was drifting into unconsciousness each time and prodded him awake again.

At four-thirty he got up, dressed quickly, then stealthily climbed through his bedroom window into the cold dewy air of a misty, fretful morning. He shivered, as much from nervousness as from the chill.

But now, breathless and weak from dragging his bundle across two fields, he was sweating. The mist had soon cleared, leaving the sun shining from a cloudless sky. William was glad he would be on the beach in a few moments. Then his bundle could be blown up and the rest of the journey to the seal would be easy.

He struggled up the meadow bank to the cliff edge.

"Oh, heck!" he said aloud as soon as he saw the sea.

He had entirely forgotten the tide.

His plan supposed that the sea would be no higher up the beach than when Gwyn took him to the cave yesterday. But that had been later in the day, when the tide was almost as far out as it went. Now the sea covered the sand where he and Gwyn had played, and was furling among the pebbles. Which was bound to mean he could not wade across to the cave. The water would be too deep.

William looked anxiously around while his mind raced. How long would it be before the sea was far enough out to wade through? How long would it be before Gwyn came to check the seal? Would Gwyn get here before the sea was shallow enough? Everything depended on William reaching the cave and rescuing the seal before Gwyn arrived to stop him or to see where William took the pup.

William's idea was to wade to the cave pulling an inflatable dinghy behind him. He had found the little blow-up boat in the junk shop. It was the sort people played with in swimming pools, an imitation of the proper ones used by airmen when they crashed into the sea. William intended getting the seal some-how—he still wasn't quite sure how—into the dinghy which he would then tow along the shore well away from the cave, till he found a suitable place to hide the pup. Another cave maybe, but certainly some-where unvisited that Gwyn wouldn't think of searching.

The pup could stay there until it wanted to go to sea. After all, William argued to himself, if the pup's mother had deserted what did it matter where the pup lived till its time came to swim away? So long as the place was not disturbed by people.

But he would have to do all this before Gwyn turned up. Last night the plan had seemed fool-proof, neat and sound, and easier every time he thought of it. This morning, as he looked at the sea surging gently seventy feet below, his plan seemed anything but foolproof and far from easy. And difficult questions he had not thought of in the junk shop kept popping into his mind.

Suddenly he felt very lonely. He breathed in deeply to keep his stomach from heaving. Whatever he felt, he was still sure of one thing: no matter what happened, he was going to rescue that seal. There could be no turning back.

William took another deep breath. There was no point in hanging about on this cliff top. He was too visible. Someone might see him. His father going off to fish. Mr Davies perhaps. And that would be that: no rescue today or any day.

He picked up his bundle and went sliding and slithering down the cliff to the beach. He did not dare tumble the bundle down on its own because he was afraid a jagged stone might tear the dinghy's plastic skin. He wouldn't be able to blow it up at all then.

On the beach William stood for a moment surveying the sea. The water was flat calm. With the sun shining brightly from behind him, and with no breeze yet, everything was warm, peaceful, quiet. Except for the slur of slow waves scouring the pebbles. There weren't even any seagulls crying.

He began untying the bundle. Yesterday afternoon he had practised blowing the dinghy up. He had managed in just over a quarter of an hour of hard work, using a bicycle pump from one of the old bikes. Now, as he laid out the wrinkled skin, William decided that what he would do, as the tide was so high, was paddle the dinghy to the cave. He ought to be able to do that without trouble. And maybe by the time he got the seal aboard, the tide would be low enough for him to wade back, as he had planned, towing the dinghy behind him.

He sat down, legs spread apart on either side of the dinghy skin at the place where the nipple of the air valve was fixed. He attached the bicycle pump and began blowing.

Slowly—much slower, he was certain, than yesterday—the boat began taking shape, like a small bathtub with a fat tyre for walls.

When he had done at last, the dinghy firm and
balloon bouncy, William glanced at his wrist watch.
Ten minutes past six. His arms were aching from the
effort. And he was feeling very hungry. He wished
he had been able to eat breakfast before he set off,
but that would have woken his parents.

He had to force himself on. Gwyn was sure to be
up and about soon. Farmers started early in the day.
He guessed that by seven o'clock Gwyn would be
free to come to the cave, and it would take William
all the time he had till then to do what had to be
done.

He was glad to see that the water was a foot or
two farther down the beach than it had been when
he arrived. The sandy strip was beginning to show.

William tugged off his shoes and socks, stowed
them in the dinghy's carrying bag with the pump,
and hid the bag behind a big boulder at the base of
the cliff.

He had brought a couple of hand paddles with
him and a length of nylon rope. These he put into
the dinghy, then pulled the boat carefully across the
beach and into the sea. Its balloony weight rode on
the surface as slippily as a bar of soap on ice.

This was the point of no return. William took in
a deep breath, let it out in a long sigh, checked
behind him that no one was watching, and thought,
"Seal pup, here I come."

He almost threw himself into the boat, stomach
down. The dinghy bobbed away seawards at an

alarming speed. William hurriedly pushed his hands through the straps of the hand-paddles, and began scooping at the water.

At first the dinghy was hard to control. All William succeeded in doing was to turn in a crazy kind of circle that took him farther out to sea. Going in a straight line was the last thing the boat wanted to do. But after a few strokes, he found that with just the right strength in each he could keep the boat headed towards the cave.

Soon he was paddling with a steady rhythm. At each surge forward water slapped against the bow and sometimes sprayed into his face. It was like swimming the breast-stroke without his body being in the water.

William began to enjoy the journey, pleased by his unexpected skill. He found himself wishing his father could see him doing so well. Maybe when the rescue was over, he would get his father to come to the beach and surprise him with a demonstration.

William's anxieties left him. He felt light-headed, confident; and the more confident he felt the quicker and more smoothly he managed to force the boat onward.

But as he rounded the bluff and entered the inlet, William noticed he was making slower progress, even though he was paddling as hard as ever. It was as though someone was pushing against the boat. To his left the island seemed to loom much bigger than it seemed from the shore.

He realized that the tide, funnelling out of the inlet and passing either side of the island, must be stronger here than along the open beach. If he stopped paddling he would be swept out to sea, or worse, wrecked on the rocky island.

Not a happy thought. William pushed it from his mind. Keeping his eyes fixed on his goal, he tried not to lose the steady rhythm of his strokes, even though the sea was rougher now. The boat wanted to slip and bob as each wave humped beneath it. He had to guess quickly what it would do next and how to keep it on course.

The hard work brought him out in a sweat. His mouth was dry and stiff-jawed. For a while he thought he was making no headway at all. Paddling became a dull, painful, mechanical movement. His arms ached. In his head he was pleading with himself to stop, just for a minute. But he knew if he did he would be dragged backwards by the tide. And any distance lost would be all the harder to make up again.

So he forced himself to keep going. And then when it seemed he really was getting nowhere, he saw that the cave was coming closer and closer, and that each stroke brought him nearer still.

At last, with a few extra-strong thrusts with the paddles, William managed to beach the dinghy in the cave mouth. He jumped ashore, pulled the boat out of the water, and slumped down on to the sand.

Never before had he felt such relief. Solid ground

beneath him. An end to the grinding ache in his arms. The first stage of the rescue successfully finished. William smiled to himself.

When he had caught his breath, he sat up and looked across the water at the island and the long line of beach. The beach looked much farther away than it had seemed yesterday. He wondered how he had dared paddle across.

For a moment William felt twinges of guilt. Everyone—his father, his mother, Mr Davies, Miss James, even Gwyn—would say he had done something wrong. He knew that. He knew what he had done was dangerous. But he could not help revelling in his success.

Besides, William told himself, he had done it for the seal. He had no choice about it: he had to save the pup.

He got up, checked that the dinghy was safe from being washed away by any unusually high wave, and stepped quietly into the cave.

12

This time William had no trouble seeing the pup. It was lying just where it had been yesterday. Gwyn must have worked on the wall after William left, for it was two or three layers of rock higher.

William looked at his watch. Six forty-five. No time to lose. This part of his plan he had thought out carefully, so he could work quickly. He began lifting rocks from the centre of the wall, throwing them away to his left. Soon he had made a gap wide enough to walk through.

His next job was to clear a path between the seal and the dinghy.

All along he had known that moving the seal would be the most difficult part of the rescue. William's first idea had been to carry the pup to the boat. But now, looking again at that roly-poly body, he knew he could not even lift it, never mind carry it twenty feet or more.

The pup was at least three feet long. But though it could twist a little and flap about with its flippers, he could see the pup was still too heavy for its own strength. And he knew it would not be able to turn and bite him, as long as he stayed behind its head.

William squatted on his haunches, his face as close to the pup's as he dared.

"It's all right," he said softly. "I'm not going to hurt you."

The pup wriggled and snarled and began weeping.

"You might as well make up your mind," William went on, "I'm going to get you into that boat, and take you somewhere safe. Okay?"

The pup's eyes streamed tears. And the more it snapped and yowled and stretched its mouth, displaying its sharp teeth, the more the tears swamped its eyes.

"You're very beautiful, aren't you," William said, meaning it, "and I don't blame you for getting into a temper. But I've got to move you. For your own good."

He stood up, and scratched his head in thought.

"You're too heavy to pick up, you see," he said. "And I daren't get near your front end. So I'm going to pull you down to the dinghy by your back flippers."

The pup snorted, as if clearing its nose.

"I wouldn't like it either," William said. "But I can't think of any other way." He paused, turning to look at the dinghy. "Trouble is," he said, "how do I get you in once we've reached the boat?"

During his long afternoon in the junk shop William had not been able to sort out this detail. He had hoped a solution would turn up when he was in the cave. But he still could not find one.

He sat on the wall, pondering the difficulty. With the dinghy lying on the ground, he would somehow have to lift the seal to get it over the boat's side.

Even if he could do that, he would then have to drag the boat, laden with the heavy pup, across the sand and into the sea. With the tide going out, that distance was growing longer every minute. What if the dinghy wouldn't move at all? What if it snagged on a sharp rock?

William got up and went to the cave entrance. If only, he thought, there was a hole in the beach where the sea came, like a miniature dry dock. He could put the boat in and roll the seal off the sand into the boat.

But there was no such ready-made dock along the water's edge.

He stared out across the waves at the beach beyond, watching for any sign of movement. Frustration worried at his nerves. Well, he thought, gritting his teeth, if there wasn't a place to sink the dinghy below ground level, he must dig one.

He must dig as close to the sea as he could get, where the cave floor dipped fairly steeply. He could make a hole, put the dinghy into it, get the seal into the dinghy and then dig a channel from the dinghy to the sea's edge. And he must dig where the tide had been. The sand there would be so wet and slippy that the dinghy ought to slide safely and easily into the water.

Before he had finished thinking this out, William

had selected the spot and was down on his knees scooping out sand with his bare hands. But this was a painful way of trenching. The sand rasped his skin and dug into his nails. It was slow too.

He looked for a make-shift spade. His eyes picked out the paddles. Just right. He snatched one up and began ploughing out a bath-tub shaped trench. Kneeling on the ground, legs spread apart, he scooped the sand behind him, like a dog digging a hole for a bone.

Very quickly, he excavated a dry dock. Panting, his arm muscles aching again, he slipped the dinghy into it. The boat fitted snugly, gunwales just a couple of inches below the level of the beach. Exactly as he wanted. But he must hurry now because, even as he watched, water seeped in and the sides of the hole began to crumble. Soon the boat would rise above ground level, floating on a soggy bed of sand.

He ran to the pup, which hissed its warning cry as he approached.

"Can't mess about," William said, breathless. "Got to get you in the boat. Not much time."

This was the moment he had been dreading. Not because he might be bitten, but because he would upset the seal and harm it.

"I don't know!" he said to the pup as he gathered his strength. "Seems to me putting something right can hurt as much as doing something wrong."

He glanced back at the dinghy. Already the gunwales were level with the ground.

"We've got to go," William said. "So look out."

He was talking, he knew, as much to keep up his own courage as to calm the pup.

He rubbed his hands down his jeans to clean them of sand, placed himself behind the pup, and took a deep breath.

He bent, took the pup's two back flippers, one in each of his hands. Their bony fleshiness felt like fingers in skinny gloves.

He dug in his heels and pulled.

The pup slid towards him with such unexpected ease that before William knew what was happening he slumped on to his bottom on the sand, the seal between his spread-eagled legs.

For one shocked second, William and the seal did not move. Then both came to their senses at once.

As William scrambled for safety out of range of its jaws, the pup started thrashing about as hard as it could, churning sand with its front flippers, lashing the ground with its hind ones, while trying at the same time to twist its bulky body so that it could snap at anything in reach. Tears poured from its glorious wide eyes, making trails in the fur of its face; and it screamed as if murder were being done.

"By heck!" William said, laughing despite his anxieties. "A sausage gone berserk!"

Somehow, the pup's exploding anger made it easier for William to do what he must. Moving fast and as firmly as he could, he grasped the seal's hind flippers again and hauled. He knew this time how much weight he had to pull, was prepared for the animal to come slithering towards him.

The pup went on fighting. But its first furious resistance was spent. It tried to dig its fore-flippers into the sand and would have squirmed from William's grasp, but the sand was too dry and loose. William managed to hang on.

"Pack it in," he said between pulls. "You don't want to do circus tricks do you?" He hauled again. "Or be kept for meat . . ." Another pull. "Or be caged in a zoo . . ." Pull. "And never go to sea . . ." Pull. "And never meet other seals . . ." He was panting again now. "I'm helping you escape . . ." Pull. Swallow. Deep breath. Pull. "I'm rescuing you . . ." Pull. "Can't you see that . . ." Pull. "You ungrateful beast . . ."

One more effort, the strength draining from his limbs, his hands finding it almost too much to hang on against the seal's tussling, and the pup was lying with its tail end almost against the dinghy's bow.

William let go and sat on the sand. Foolishly, he saw at once. For the seal wanted no rest. It began ploughing its way back up the beach. The sand was firmer here where the tide had been, not soft and loose as it was round the pup's nest. So its flippers found a grip and the seal began land-swimming back to the only home it had ever known.

"Hey, no you don't!" William shouted, scrambling to his feet and grabbing the seal's hind flippers again.

For a moment William and the seal played tug-of-war before he was able to drag the pup back to the boat. This time he held on tight while he caught his breath and took stock.

Getting the pup into the dinghy would be hard enough. But when he got it into the boat, would the pup go on struggling? Would it puncture the boat's plastic skin? Would it be able to push itself out of the dinghy even before they were in the water?

His carefully laid plan seemed full of difficulties he had not foreseen. For the first time, William wished there was someone else there to help him.

The thought reminded him of Gwyn. He glanced at his watch. Twenty minutes after seven. Where had all the time gone! He flushed with panic.

He turned and looked towards the shore. The first thing he saw was the unmistakable figure of Gwyn running along the beach.

13

No time left for thinking. The seal must take its chance and William with it.

He stood up, still clinging on to the pup's hind flippers, stepped backwards into the dinghy, and pulled the seal gently towards him. A few inches at a time, he dragged the seal off the sand, across the boat's cushioning gunwale and into the boat. There was no room for them both. So as the last of the seal slipped in, William stepped out, and let it go.

The pup fitted neatly inside the dinghy. There was enough room for it to lie comfortably, held by the gunwale, without there being enough space for it to flop about.

William watched to see how the pup took to its new surroundings. Luckily it seemed to like them, Maybe the softness of the inflated plastic pleased it; maybe the strangeness of being in the boat gave it enough to think about. Whatever the reason, the pup stayed calm and quiet.

Hoping it would stay like that for a while, William applied himself to his next problem: digging out a slipway down which he could pull the dinghy and its heavy load into the sea. Using a paddle, he swiftly excavated a channel. As he worked, water seeped into his trench. He was glad: the dinghy would slide more easily.

The channel made, he stood up and stared landward again. Gwyn was still there, peering back at William across the dividing sea. He waved briskly. But he was too far away for William to decide what his signals meant.

Nor did it matter. William had to get the seal away but he could not go back along the beach. He would have to find a hiding place in the other direction.

William turned back to the dinghy. The pup was warily sniffing out its new resting place. But as soon as William started dragging the boat down the slipway, the pup let out its usual loud hissing snarls, and began banging its flippers on the bottom of the boat so hard William was afraid the plastic skin would burst.

"Oh, pack it in!" he spluttered, his fear finding an outlet in blustering words. But the seal went on thrashing about.

And now the sea faced him, looking suddenly no friend of his. A fresh breeze had sprung up, curling waves on the water, and bringing garbled shouts from Gwyn.

"... ack ..." reached him, and a word that sounded like ". . .ool . . ."

William paid no attention. Resolutely he walked into the sea towing the boat behind him. The dinghy

(89)

rode well, was caught by the current and went gliding past William till it was wallowing at the end of its short painter as though wanting to break free.

The pup felt the strange new motion, raised its nose and sniffed the air. Spray fell over it. The seal shook its head like a dog and its whole body started trembling, whether from excitement or fright William could not tell. But he smiled, because he trembled in exactly the same way whenever he was going into the sea for the first time each holiday.

He glanced across the water again. Gwyn was wading into the sea, trying to get across to the cave. But he was already up to his waist so the water must still be too deep. Did that mean it would be too deep in the direction William was taking?

His heart thumped at the thought. He certainly couldn't swim and pull the dinghy at the same time. Even without the boat in tow, he doubted if he could swim far. Not with the sea breaking in choppy little waves and the strong under-surface currents he could feel swirling around his legs. Even where he was standing now waves were rising and falling between his knees and his waist. He wouldn't want to chance them getting higher.

Cautiously William set off, the dinghy's painter wrapped tightly in his left hand, his other arm held out to help keep his balance. He knew he must not cling too closely to the cliff because the sea was breaking white against it. He might get swamped in all that churning foam and sloshing water. But neither dare he go out too far, because the ground might slope away and leave him without a footing.

So he edged seawards, but carefully, searching out each step with his foot to make sure there was firm ground to stand on.

Progress was slow. The dinghy danced about, giving annoying tugs on its painter as the waves tossed it about. William had to work hard to keep himself calm and patient.

But he could not stop that awful memory coming back to him of his father egging him on to take a plunge, and then stepping away when William did as he was told and threw himself towards his father's outstretched arms.

The memory weakened his resolve. He felt his determination seeping from him. He paused and drew in a deep, sea-tangy breath. The air cooled his burning chest. But his mouth was sour and dry. He was shivering with cold and, he admitted to himself, fear too.

Gwyn, he saw, was back on the beach, and watching. He was shading his eyes with his hand. This time he did not wave or shout. Maybe, William thought ruefully, if he had been patient, he could have talked Gwyn out of his secret plan. That would have been better than this sick-making rescue. And then he would still have had Gwyn to spend his holiday with. Even if he didn't like Gwyn much, it was better to have someone to be with than no one at all.

How he wished he had someone with him now! For a brief moment he thought of turning back, of taking the seal to the cave, and paddling the dinghy across to Gwyn, and trying to explain what had happened and why.

But the next moment he knew this was impossible. Gwyn would never understand. And, William gloomily told himself once more, he had set out to save the seal and he could not give up now, no matter what.

It was then that several things happened at the same time.

William took a step forward. As he did so, the dinghy went surging past him. As if rising to meet the dinghy, a fully grown seal's head bobbed out of the water a few feet away, like a swimmer taking his bearings.

Both events startled William: the dinghy startled him out of his dark thoughts; and the seal startled him by its sudden and unexpected appearance.

At the same moment the baby seal caught sight of the new arrival, and this sent the pup into a struggling frenzy more violent than anything William had yet witnessed.

William was quite sure the pup would tear the dinghy's skin. So he plunged recklessly towards the dinghy to try and hold it still.

But his feet found nothing but water. Instinctively, William grabbed for the boat. His hands caught the gunwale. He held on for dear life. Frantic, he trod water, trying to touch bottom, but even with his legs at full stretch and his chin at water level he could not.

All the time the pup was flapping and twisting inside the boat, making the little craft lurch about, so that it was all the harder for William to hang on.

Already the sea felt different: heavier somehow, stronger. And the dinghy was rising and falling in a way that William knew meant it was drifting seawards fast.

Desperate, he pulled himself violently upwards, at the same time thrusting downwards with his legs just as he would to pull himself out of a swimming pool. As he rose out of the water he flung himself across the dinghy's gunwale. He hoped to lie there half in and half out of the dinghy, while he decided what to do.

But he had forgotten that the seal was head-on towards him. As he pulled upwards the dinghy's bow dipped under his weight. The seal slid down, and as William flung himself over the gunwale, the pup snapped with its jaws. It managed to bite him once, firmly on his left arm.

The pain was so sharp William screamed and tore his arm away. He saw blood stream from the wound.

The boat went on tipping into the water. A wave rode by. Water swirled into the dinghy. The seal flapped, caught the surging water, and almost somersaulted itself into the sea.

With the seal's weight thrown out, and the wave

passed by, the dinghy bobbed up again, somehow scooping William up with it, so that he found himself tumbling into the dinghy. Instinctively, he hung on with his unhurt hand and managed to keep himself inside.

He was safe. But the seal was gone. Holding his wounded arm close to his body, he sat up and swept the surrounding water with his eyes. The baby seal was not far away, floating low in the water like a soggy seaside toy, only the top of its podgy back showing. The adult seal was not far away, still interestedly watching William and the boat, and paying no heed to the pup. Then a wave that was bigger than most obscured William's view. When it had gone by both seals had disappeared.

William searched again and again for another sight of the pup. But it was gone. The rescue was over. In the end the seal had taken care of itself. He need not have troubled himself. All he need have done was slip the pup into the sea at the cave mouth, and it would have swum away, saving itself from Gwyn's plan.

A rough wave went by, the dinghy swirled in its wake, turning so that William was facing seaward. The movement brought him back to himself and his predicament.

He saw at once, and with a renewed sickening panic, what his fate was to be. The island loomed ahead. He was approaching at a startling speed. Already he could hear waves smashing against it.

Unless he did something quickly, he knew he must end up there, wrecked on its sharp and rocky cliffs.

He lay flat down on his stomach so that he could paddle with his hands on either side of the boat. But as soon as he tried to use his left arm, the pain from the seal pup's bite made him flinch away from the water. He kept trying with his right hand. But the drift towards the island was so strong, his puny strokes were useless.

A few seconds later the dinghy lurched. William heard a hiss of escaping air and the boat began to deflate beneath him. Like a punctured tyre, it collapsed into a slippery bundle of wet, wrinkled plastic that left William floundering in the sea.

His nightmare was coming true. Water swallowed him into itself. But his head was hardly covered before a rising wave took him in its grip. He fought against it, thrashing with his arms and legs to free himself. But there was no escape. The wave bowled him over and over, sucked him down, threw him up, and broke with him in its clasp against the jagged and seaweed-slimy rocks of the island's rugged side.

14

How he got to the top of the island William never knew.

First he heard the sea surging, breaking, slapping on the chiselled rocks thirty feet below. He opened his eyes, saw sharp, clear blue, tingling with sunlight. His spread-eagled hands clutched short, spiky grass.

He remembered being wrecked. It was like coming out of an awful dream, a terrifying nightmare, and finding it was true after all.

And then he felt the pain. A sharp burning pain in his left leg. A pain that made his eyes water. And cleared his head.

He tried moving his leg. The pain became a cry in his mouth, a scream. He had never felt anything so frightening. Not even when his mother closed the car door too suddenly one day and caught William's fingers in it. He had wept for over an hour. But that pain had been only in his fingers. This was much much worse. It filled the whole of his body.

He sighed, trying to breathe the pain out of himself. Could he sit up, he wondered? He wanted to know exactly where he was, wanted to find out why his leg hurt so badly.

Carefully, waiting for that torturing stab in his leg to flash through him, he propped himself up on his right hand.

His left leg looked strange. The bottom part, below the knee, was sticking out at an odd angle. He found it hard to think of the leg as his own. And the last thing he wanted to do was touch it.

He lifted his head and gazed across the inlet to the coast. He could see the dark hole of the cave, and along from the cave, the beginning of the beach. And on the beach he could see a small figure.

Gwyn? It had to be Gwyn. He was watching, looking towards William perched on the island's grass-cushioned top. Gwyn had to help. He was William's only hope.

William bent forward so that he could use his right hand to get off his shirt. The cloth was still damp and stuck to him. Where the wound was on his left arm, blood had clotted, sticking the torn shirt sleeve to his skin. But he got it off, braced himself, and waved the flapping shirt above his head.

After only five or six flaps, his arm was aching. He had to rest. But he watched fixedly the figure on the beach.

Gwyn did not move.

William flapped his shirt again, more desperately this time, trying to raise himself off the ground, till his leg shot such an agonizing pain through him, that he fell back vomiting a scream again.

When he could look once more Gwyn was no

longer standing on the beach. William searched along the shore and then the cliff and picked Gwyn out at last from the rocks and stones of the cliff side, as he scrambled up.

William tried not even to blink in case he lost sight of Gwyn again. He watched as Gwyn reached the cliff top, turned, and looked in William's direction.

William clutched his shirt, raised it above him, and waved.

But this time he only waved once. For then Gwyn set off, running along the cliff top, not in the direction of the farm or the cottage, but away from home. Away from help.

"Gwyn!" William shouted.

But shouting was no use. He knew that. Gwyn was too far off; William's voice would be lost in the ceaseless sounds of the sea.

Surely Gwyn was not going to leave him here? Surely he would get help? But there was only beach and cliff and fields grazed by cattle and sheep where Gwyn was going. No one who could do anything.

Maybe Gwyn did not realize how hurt William was? Maybe he thought William was resting and could swim back?

No, that was not it. He was angry because William had freed the seal. But if Gwyn knew how badly hurt William was, would he do nothing? Nobody could be that cruel. No matter how angry they were. Could they?

William wanted to tell himself no, they couldn't. But he knew it was not true. People were always being cruel to each other. The news on television was full of such things. People planting bombs in all sorts of places so that they would kill and hurt other people when they exploded. Men who burst into houses and shot people who did not agree with them. People, even, who stabbed each other just because they supported different sides at football matches.

The seal pup had been just as important to Gwyn as a football team was to other boys.

If people disagreed it seemed they could do anything to each other, even the most horrible things. Were people only friends, really friends, when they thought alike? When they agreed about the things that were very important to them? Could he and Gwyn have been friends even though they did not agree about the seal?

He lay back on the grass. He could not think about that now. It was all too difficult. His leg was throbbing as though a pump was beating inside it. All that really mattered now was that he was alone on this island and too hurt to escape.

He closed his eyes. In his head he saw the figure of Gwyn running along the cliff top. Running the wrong way.

He wished he could forget it. Forget everything. Be back home. Safe. In his own bed. Comfortable. Warm.

The sun was warm on him now. Soothing. And

the grass was soft under him. Not hard like the rocks. The breeze cooled him. Flies buzzed by now and then. Sea-gulls called their sad lonely cries. And all the time, all the time the sea, washing the rocks.

The sound of the sea surging beyond his feet was the last thing William heard as he slipped into sleep.

15

When he woke William decided he must be dying.

He felt so ill he was sure he was dying. No one could feel so sick and not die. Besides, he was alone. There was no one to help. Gwyn had run away. His father and mother would not know where he was. Miss James was in Bristol. There was no one to rescue him. He was bound to die.

William had not thought about dying before. Not dying like this. Not about death happening to *him*, here, *now*. Though he was sweating from the heat of the sun, shining from high in the sky, he went cold inside. Goose-pimples broke out, their little pin-heads erupting all over his skin.

He shivered. He tried moving his leg, but the pain went scorching through him worse than before and the throbbing below his knee started up again.

It was best to lie still and die quietly.

What happened to you when you died, William wondered. Some people said you went to heaven. Mr Powell at school said you went to heaven and read bits from the Bible about it. But William always had the greatest difficulty imagining what heaven was like. He had asked Mr Powell to describe it for him. And Mr Powell had had difficulty too. He said a lot about what it was not like, but very little about what it was like. Heaven, Mr Powell said, was inside you. But when William asked whereabouts inside you, Mr Powell told him not to be cheeky.

William sighed. His lips and mouth were parched and his throat felt like it would crack. He longed for a drink. All that water only a few yards away, but none of it any good!

Dying wasn't going to be very pleasant. He hoped it would happen fast. He wouldn't mind if it happened quickly and without much pain. He wasn't very good about pain. He never had been and he doubted if he ever would be. He didn't like pain and that was all he could say.

Some people seemed not to mind it. Bert Simpson at school, for instance. He had run up against a wall during a chase in the playground and had hit his knee so hard that the skin split open and blood gushed out. Bert was taken to hospital where they put five stitches in the cut. Bert's knee had been bandaged for days afterwards, and he limped about using a stick specially cut down to his size from one of his grandfather's old ones. But all the time, even when it happened, Bert never screamed or cried or even winced much. He kept smiling and saying it was all right and nothing really.

William had wondered at the time whether he could ever be as brave as Bert Simpson. Now he knew he couldn't. Pain finished him.

A fly settled on his forehead. Its legs tickled him as it walked about. William tried to brush it away with his good hand. He was amazed how difficult it was to raise his hand to his head. All his strength had gone. His hand flopped weakly to his side again.

Another thing he would hate about dying, William thought, was that he would never know now what it was like to be grown up. He had been looking forward to growing up for ages, to having his own house, and being able to go places and do things when he wanted and how he wanted, and not when adults told him he must or how he should.

One of the things he liked about Gwyn, even though he hated so many other things, was that Gwyn wanted to be grown up too. He wanted to have his own herd of cows and his own farm and to get on doing things properly. He wasn't just playing about.

Colin Pearce, who lived next door to William, wasn't like that at all. Colin said he never wanted to be grown up because grown-ups had all the hard work to do. They had to earn money to live on, and look after their children, mend their houses and repair their cars and keep up appearances. Colin's mother was always going on about keeping up appearances. Colin said that one thing he was not going to do when he grew up was keep up appearances. It sounded far too boring and too much hard work.

"Mind you," Colin had said, "if I had parents like yours, I'd probably want to be grown up too."

But his parents weren't as bad as all that, William decided now that he thought about it as he was dying. They were only trying to do their best, and, really, he would miss them when he was dead. In fact, he admitted to himself, he missed them now, before he was dead. If only they were here perhaps he would not have to die at all.

He would miss his room, too, and drawing and his books, and he would miss coming to the seaside every year. Even though the sea had been the cause of his death.

He felt very sad about dying. So sad that tears swam in his eyes and flooded them till they overflowed and trickled down past his ears and into his hair. He made no effort to stop them. All the time, from the moment he set off this morning till he was wrecked on the island, he had not wept. He had felt like it sometimes. When he couldn't think how to get the seal into the dinghy, he had felt like it. And when the seal disappeared into the waves. He had felt like crying then more than at any other time. But he hadn't.

Now though, if he was going to die alone and before he was grown up and properly himself, he thought he had a right to cry. He wanted to, and anyway, there was no one to see him.

As his tears flowed, William felt as if he were floating, drifting away calmly in the warm sunlight.

His leg was numb; he could hardly feel any pain in it. His arm, where the seal had bitten it, was stiff and sore, but no longer hurt either. And his head felt muggy. Thinking was becoming difficult. All he wanted to do was close his eyes and sleep again.

16

William was woken by the angel of death. He knew it was the angel of death because it came in a storm of wind and a loud noise of beating wings. The wind was almost strong enough to bowl him over and over; he had to brace himself against the ground. And the roar of its wings was so great it nearly deafened him.

He opened his eyes. The angel of death was a helicopter with a fat yellow belly hovering above him, its wings whirring in a wide flashing circle. From it was dropping a space man. He came very fast and landed a few feet from William's head. He unbuckled himself from a harness that attached him to a line, then waved up at the helicopter, which slid away in a steep banking turn, rising into the blue sky as it went.

Wind and noise went with it, leaving a calm so silent William had to listen hard to hear that the sea was still there beneath him washing the cliffs.

"How are you, son?" a voice said.

William turned his head and saw a man's face looking at him from inside a fish-bowl helmet. For a moment he thought he had forgotten how to speak.

No words would come. It was as though the words were trapped in his mind.

"Are you," he struggled to say at last, "are you the Air Sea Rescue?" His voice surprised him: it did not sound like his own. It rasped and was deeper than it should be.

"That's what I am," the man said. "And you're a lucky fellow."

"I . . . I . . ." William was not stammering this time. What he wanted to tell this man was how he had rescued a seal. He wanted to tell him that was why he, William, was marooned here on this island with a hurt leg. He wanted to tell him he was proud of rescuing the seal, even though he had not made a very good job of it. He was sure that someone who rescued people would understand and would be pleased William had tried to save the seal.

But something stopped the words from getting as far as his mouth. Something was clutching them in his head.

Then he remembered. The oath. He had promised Gwyn never, not for any reason at all, to mention the seal to anyone.

"You what?" the man said. He was a kindly man with a smile. William liked him and liked him most of all for being here now.

"I . . . I think my leg is hurt," William said.

The man moved out of William's sight. But he felt the man touching his leg. The pain jabbed through him again, and he cried out.

"You've broken it," the man said.

Then he touched the very place that was the centre of the hurt and the pain was so suddenly fierce, so striking, like the sudden sharp stab of a red hot knife, that the world disappeared.

17

"It's all my fault," Miss James said. "I should have got rid of that silly dinghy years ago. It was only a toy really, not suitable for the sea." She sighed. "Thank goodness you're safe."

She was sitting beside William in the cottage garden. William's left leg was covered from foot to thigh in plaster. It stuck out in front of him, his foot resting on an upturned box. Miss James did not seem able to take her eyes off it.

Miss James had arrived from Bristol only a few minutes before and wanted to hear the whole story immediately. William told her what he told everyone: that he had gone out early to play with the dinghy, that he had got caught by the tide, been swept away, and wrecked on the island. No lies, just the part about the seal missed out. So he had not broken his oath.

"What a lucky thing Gwyn spotted you," Miss James said.

William smiled, hoping this would end the conversation. But Miss James went on, "What a pity, though, you had to spend most of your holiday in hospital."

"I didn't mind," William said. He hadn't either. The nurses spoilt him. The other kids in the ward, mostly there because of boring ailments like appendicitis and tonsils, treated him like a hero. His adventure had been the talk of the place. A reporter from the local newspaper had interviewed him, and there had been a photograph of William propped up in bed with the Air Sea Rescue man who saved him sitting by his side.

All of which made up for the pain in his leg, and the telling-off he got from his father as soon as he was fit enough to listen. His leg hurt still, in a dull sort of way. Not enough to complain about but enough to be wearying. The worst thing now was that the skin under the plaster itched, nearly driving William mad because there was no way he could scratch. The doctor said he would have to wear the plaster for twelve weeks.

"Dad's making a bonfire," William said, changing the subject.

"Oh, how nice," Miss James said. "To celebrate your return home?"

"Because it's our last night here."

William's mother came round the side of the cottage pushing a wheelbarrow with cushions in it. She set it down at William's side.

"Your dad's lit the fire," she said. "And Mr Davies is there with Gwyn."

"Sounds like a party," Miss James said. "Don't you think William's been very brave?"

"He's been very daft if you ask me," William's mother said. She helped William hop from the chair into the wheelbarrow. He winced when his leg jarred inside the plaster. "Still," his mother said, ruffling his hair, "he's all we've got, so I suppose we'll have to put up with him." She laughed. "Have you given Miss James your present?"

"A present!" Miss James said. "For me?"

"I did it in hospital," William said. He hated moments like this. "I had to pass the time somehow."

"Where is it?" his mother asked.

"In my room. On top of the drawers."

"I can't wait," Miss James said, standing up. "Shall I get it? I've got to go in anyway and change into something more relaxed for the party."

She hurried off into the cottage. William's mother trundled William round to the back of the cottage where the stock yard used to be. In the middle of the yard Mr Davies, Gwyn and William's father were standing round a huge bonfire made of rubbish from the junk shop. The fire had just been lit; flames were already blazing and smoke was billowing thickly into the evening sky.

"I'll not take you too near in case you get burnt," William's mother said, stopping well away from the fire. "I'm going in to fetch us all some drinks. Will you be all right?"

William nodded. His mother left him. Mr Davies turned and waved.

"Glad you're home, boy," he called.

William's father said something; Mr Davies laughed and turned back to the fire.

Gwyn wandered across, smiling—smugly, William thought. Gwyn had not visited William in hospital: this was the first time they had met since the rescue.

"Want my autograph for your leg?" Gwyn said.

"Haven't got a pen," William said.

"Does it hurt?"

"No."

"I never broke anything," Gwyn said.

"You should try it sometime."

"Ha-ha," Gwyn said.

William did not take his eyes from the burning junk.

"You're a bit of a cloth-head, Billy-boy," Gwyn said. "Couldn't you see you'd get in trouble?"

William smiled. "I rescued the seal, that's all."

Gwyn laughed as if William had made a joke. "There's brave!" he said. "But there's more where that one come from. And you'll not be here to-morrow."

William could say nothing. Gwyn's irrepressible cockiness angered him. And knowing he would not be able to stop Gwyn carrying out his plan.

"You should be grateful," Gwyn said. "I saved your life, didn't I? Yes."

"Thanks very much," William said as acidly as he could.

"Never mind. I come out of it nicely."

William couldn't guess what Gwyn meant, but he would not ask.

"I thought you'd like to know," Gwyn said after waiting for William's question. "My da gave me a calf. Good, eh?"

"Gave you? What for?"

"Telling the coast-guard about you, of course. Initiative, my da says. Using my head in an emergency. Being sensible."

William's anger showed; he couldn't help it. "You think that's smart, don't you? You took the calf, but I bet you never thought of telling about the seal and about what really happened, did you?"

Gwyn guffawed exaggeratedly. "*Me* tell! I'm not daft, boy!"

Miss James appeared, bearing William's picture carefully before her.

"William, it's wonderful," she said. "Marvellous. I'm very touched. I really am. Isn't it lovely, Gwyn?" She showed the picture. It was not of the cottage. In hospital, William could not recall it well enough to get the details right. What he could remember in the smallest detail was the baby seal. He had drawn the pup and painted it: a baby seal lying on sand and surrounded by rocks and sea-weedy pools.

"Don't you think William is talented?" Miss James said.

Gwyn grinned. "Oh, he's clever all right," he said. "A real genius."

"I do thank you, William," Miss James said. "I must get it framed. The seal is so lifelike. I suppose you must have copied it from a book? You've done it very well. There are some seals near Pentyn Head, you know." She beamed happily at William. "Maybe if you come again, Gwyn will show you them."

"I will, Miss James," Gwyn said. "Any time."

William could tell Gwyn was hardly able to stop himself giggling.

"I'm so pleased you two have become such good friends," Miss James went on, not noticing. "It's such a shame you didn't have more time together. But maybe I can persuade William's parents to bring him back next year. Good heavens, look at the bonfire! Isn't it big! I must take this painting in before the smoke damages it."

She hurried away, still exclaiming her pleasure.

The bonfire crackled, exploding sparks into the darkening sky. William watched them fade and die before they fell. As he watched, he rubbed his arm where the seal pup had bitten it. The marks were only a dull red blemish in his skin now. He hoped they would not vanish completely, but that they would always remain, like a badge, a medal, reminding him of the day he first did something important on his own, something grown-up.

Suddenly he was glad Gwyn had made him swear an oath to keep the seal secret; was glad that Gwyn himself hadn't told. Because now the memory of the rescue would be William's own, something precious to keep to himself.

The fire shot more sparks into the sky. Gwyn ran to it and began hurling rubbish into the flames.

"More, more!" William shouted. "Build it bigger!"

Gwyn and Mr Davies and William's father turned in surprise and stared at him. Then Mr Davies and William's father burst into laughter.

"By the heck," William's father said, "our lad's making himself heard at last!"

"Won't do him no harm, either," Mr Davies said, coming over to William. He took hold of the wheelbarrow and pushed William closer to the blaze.

"If you'd shown a bit more gump a few days ago," William's father said, "you might have kept yourself out of bother."

"Oh, I don't know," Mr Davies said. "From what I hear, he didn't do so bad at all. Did you, boy?"

And he gave William a very big wink.

This book
is dedicated to
Jay and Bobbie Williams
gyda chariad

Part **1** of the City Cats Series

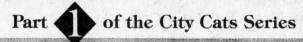

Colin Dann

King of the Vagabonds

By the creator of the award-winning
THE ANIMALS OF FARTHING WOOD

Incredible animal adventures starring
furry felines, Sammy and Pinkie...

'Don't stray into Quartermile Field. Any animal with sense avoids the spot,' warns Sammy's mother. But Sammy is curious - about the Field, and about his father, the fierce, wild father he's never met.

Then one day Sammy discovers that his father has returned. And determined to track him down, Sammy sets off towards the strange, wild land of Quartermile Field - and into a very different and dangerous world...

THE CITY CATS SERIES by Colin Dann
in paperback from Red Fox

KING OF THE VAGABONDS
ISBN 0 09 921192 0   £3.50

THE CITY CATS
ISBN 0 09 921202 1   £3.50

COPYCAT
ISBN 0 09 21212 9   £3.99

Part **2** of the City Cats Series

Colin Dann

The
City Cats

By the creator of the award-winning
THE ANIMALS OF FARTHING WOOD

Incredible animal adventures starring
furry felines, Sammy and Pinkie...

Scavenging for food in the back of a van leads Sammy and Pinkie into trouble when they suddenly find themselves trapped - and travelling. They arrive in a scary place, full of fast cars and strange people, but a park provides shelter and a fat pigeon makes a fine meal. Sammy's still the proud King of the Vagabonds and Pinkie's looking forward to having a family. As big city cats they've finally found the good life. But how long can it last...?

THE CITY CATS SERIES by Colin Dann
in paperback from Red Fox

KING OF THE VAGABONDS
ISBN 0 09 921192 0   £3.50

THE CITY CATS
ISBN 0 09 921202 1   £3.50

COPYCAT
ISBN 0 09 21212 9   £3.99

Other great reads ✦ *from* **Red Fox**

Whatever you like to read, Red Fox has got the story for you. Why not choose another book from our range of Animal Stories, Funny Stories or Fantastic Stories? Reading has never been so much fun!

Red Fox Funny Stories

THANKS FOR THE SARDINE
Laura Beaumont

Poor Aggie is sick and tired of hearing her mates jabbering on about how brilliant their Aunties are. Aggie's aunties are useless. In fact they're not just boring – they don't even try! Could a spell at Aunt Augusta's Academy of Advanced Auntiness be the answer?

Chucklesome stuff!
Young Telegraph

GIZZMO LEWIS: FAIRLY SECRET AGENT
Michael Coleman

Gizzmo Lewis, newly qualified secret agent from the planet Sigma-6, is on a mission. He's been sent to check out the defences of a nasty little planet full of ugly creatures – yep, you guessed it, he's on planet Earth! It's all a shock to Gizzmo's system so he decides to sort things out – alien-style!

0 09 926631 8   £2.99

THE HOUSE THAT SAILED AWAY
Pat Hutchins

It has rained all holiday! But just as everyone is getting really fed up of being stuck indoors, the house starts to shudder and rock, and then just floats off down the street to the sea. Hungry cannibals, bloody-thirsty pirates and a cunning kidnapping are just some of the hair-raisers in store.

0 09 993200 8   £2.99

Other great reads *from* **Red Fox**

Red Fox Fantastic Stories

THE STEALING OF QUEEN VICTORIA
Shirley Isherwood
Boo and his grandmother live above Mr Timms' antique
shop. Neither of them has paid too much attention to the old
bust of Queen Victoria which sits in the shop – until a strange
man offers them some money to steal it for him!
Compelling reading
Book for Keeps

0 09 940152 5   £2.99

THE INFLATABLE SHOP
Willis Hall
The Hollins family is off on holiday– to crummy Cockleton-
on-Sea. Some holiday! So one particularly windy, rainy day,
it's Henry Hollins' good luck that he steps into Samuel
Swain's Inflatable Shop just as a great inflatable adventure
is about to begin!
Highly entertaining
Junior Education

0 09 940162 2   £2.99

TRIV IN PURSUIT
Michael Coleman
Something very fishy is happening at St Ethelred's School.
One by one all the teachers are vanishing into thin air leaving
very odd notes behind. Triv suspects something dodgy is
happening. The search is on to solve the mind-boggling
mystery of the missing teachers.

0 09 940083 9   £2.99

AGENT Z GOES WILD
Mark Haddon
When Ben sets off on an outward bound trip with Barney and
Jenks, he should have realised there'd be crime-busting, top-
secret snooping and toothpaste-sabotaging to be done . . .
0 09 940073 1   £2.99

Other great reads ⬻ *from* **Red Fox**

Red Fox Animal Stories

FOWL PEST
(Shortlisted for the Smarties Prize)
James Andrew Hall
Amy Pickett wants to be a chicken! Seriously! Understandably her family aren't too keen on the idea. Even Amy's best friend, Clarice, thinks she's unhinged. Then Madam Marvel comes to town and strange feathery things begin to happen.
A Fantastic tale, full of jokes
Child Education
0 09 940182 7   £2.99

OMELETTE: A CHICKEN IN PERIL
Gareth Owen
As the egg breaks, a young chicken pops his head out of the crack to see, with horror, an enormous frying pan. And so Omelette is born into the world! This is just the beginning of a hazardous life for the wide-eyed chicken who must learn to keep his wits about him.
0 09 940013 8   £2.99

ESCAPE TO THE WILD
Colin Dann
Eric made up his mind. He would go to the pet shop, open the cages and let the little troupe of animals escape to the wild.
Readers will find the book unputdownable
Growing Point
0 09 940063 4   £2.99

SEAL SECRET
Aidan Chambers
William is really fed up on holliday in Wales until Gwyn, the boy from the nearby farm, shows him the seal lying in a cave. Gwyn knows exactly what he is going to do with it; William knows he has to stop him . . .
0 09 991150 0   £2.99

THE RUNTON

WEREWOLF

Ritchie Perry

*'I suppose I ought to mention one minor fact about myself -
I'm a werewolf. Yes, that's right, I'm a werewolf.
So is Dad, and my mum is a vampire...'*

By day Alan's a normal schoolboy. But at night his 'gronk factor'
kicks in - and suddenly, he's not your average kind of guy...

THE RUNTON WEREWOLF
When a legendary werewolf is spotted running through
Runton, Alan uncovers an amazing family secret - and
suddenly his hair-raising bad dreams begin to make sense...

THE RUNTON WEREWOLF
AND THE BIG MATCH
Alan's just got to grips with being a Gronk (a nice, friendly
werewolf) only to discover that a couple of mad scientists
are hot on his trail. Poor Alan - it looks like it's all over...

THE RUNTON WEREWOLF by Ritchie Perry
Red Fox *paperback*, ISBN 0 09 930327 2   £2.99

THE RUNTON WEREWOLF
AND THE BIG MATCH by Ritchie Perry,
Red Fox *paperback*, ISBN 0 09 968901 4   £3.50

ADVENTURE

The Adventure Series by Willard Price

Read these exciting stories about Hal and Roger Hunt and their search
for wild animals. Out now in paperback from Red Fox at £3.50

Amazon Adventure

Hal and Roger find themselves
abandoned and alone in the
Amazon Jungle when a mission
to explore unchartered territory
of the Pastaza River goes off course...
0 09 918221 1

Underwater Adventure

The intrepid Hunts have joined forces
with the Oceanographic Institute to
study sea life, collect specimens and
follow a sunken treasure ship trail...
0 09 918231 9

Arctic Adventure

Olrik the eskimo and his bear,
Nanook, join Hal and Roger on
their trek towards the polar ice cap.
And with Zeb the hunter hot on
their trail the temperature soon turns
from cold to murderously chilling...
0 09 918321 8

Elephant Adventure

Danger levels soar with the
temperature for Hal and Roger as they
embark upon a journey to the equator,
charged with the task of finding an
extremely rare white elephant...
0 09 918331 5

Volcano Adventure

A scientific study of the volcanoes
of the Pacific with world famous
volcanologist, Dr Dan Adams,
erupts into an adventure of a
lifetime for Hal and Roger....
0 09 918241 6

South Sea Adventure

Hal and Roger can't resist the offer
of a trip to the South Seas in search
of a creature known as the
Nightmare of the Pacific...
0 09 918251 3

Safari Adventure

Tsavo national park has become
a death trap. Can Hal and Roger
succeed in their mission of liberating
it from the clutches of a Blackbeard's
deadly gang of poachers?...
0 09 918341 2

African Adventure

On safari in African big-game
country, Hal and Roger coolly tackle
their brief to round up a mysterious
man-eating beast. Meanwhile, a
merciless band of killers follow in
their wake...
0 09 918371 4

It's wild! It's dangerous! And it's out there!